FRANKENSTEIN

According to
SPIKE MILLIGAN

Other titles available

BLACK BEAUTY ACCORDING TO
SPIKE MILLIGAN

SPIKE MILLIGAN: A CELEBRATION

FRANKENSTEIN

According to
SPIKE MILLIGAN

First published in Great Britain in 1997 by
Virgin Books
an imprint of Virgin Publishing Ltd
332 Ladbroke Grove
London W10 5AH

A catalogue record for this book is available from the British Library.

ISBN 1 85227 609 6

Typeset by TW Typesetting, Plymouth, Devon

Printed and bound by
Mackays of Chatham, Lordswood, Chatham, Kent

From acid and brine
Mixed with horses' urine
I fashioned the Frankenstein
He craves for a cigarette
So far they haven't caught him yet.

When I was very young I started to
collect bits of people
I stored them in old deserted steeples
The bits were all homeless people and
nowhere to go
To preserve them I packed them in snow.

What made me want to make such a
horror
With human bits I started to beg, steal
or borrow
One day in the spring
I would stitch it all together with string.

AUTHOR'S INTRODUCTION TO THE STANDARD NOVELS EDITION (1831)

The publishers of the Standard Novels, in selecting *Frankenstein* for one of their series, expressed a wish that I should furnish them with an account of the origin. Well my own account stands at £3.10. 'How I, then a young girl, came to think of and dilate upon so very hideous an idea?' The answer is I was kinky and pretty bent and was smoking the stuff. It is true that I am very averse to bringing myself forward in print; I would rather bring myself sideways. In writing this book, I can scarcely accuse myself of a personal intrusion; I always get someone else to do it.

It is not singular that, as the daughter of two persons of distinguished literary celebrity, I should very early in life have thought of writing, and I did. I was two. My dreams were at once more fantastic and agreeable than my writings. In the latter I was a close imitator – in other words, a little bloody cheat. What I wrote was intended at least for the human eye, so I had to look around for one-eyed readers.

I lived principally in the country as a girl and passed considerable time in Scotland. I won the Junior Women's

Haggis Hurling Championship. I discovered nothing was worn under the kilt; everything was in working order. But my residence was on the dreary northern shores of the Tay where I met the poet William McGonigal who wrote:

THE RAILWAY BRIDGE OF THE SILVERY TAY

Beautiful railway bridge of the Silvery Tay
With your numerous artists and palaces in so grand array
And your central girders which seem so high
To be almost towering to the sky
The greatest wonder of the day
And the great beautification to the River Tay
Most beautiful to be seen
Near by Dundee and the Magdalen Green.

Beautiful railway bridge of the Silvery Tay
That has caused the Emperor of Brazil to leave his home far away
Incognito in his dress
In view as he passed along en route to Inverness.

Beautiful railway bridge of the Silvery Tay
The longest of the present day
That has ever crossed over a tidal river stream
Most gigantic to be seen
Near by Dundee and the Magdalen Green.

Beautiful railway bridge of the Silvery Tay
Which will cause great celebration on the opening day
And hundreds of people will come from far away
Also the Queen most gorgeous to be seen
Near by Dundee and the Magdalen Green.

Beautiful railway bridge of the Silvery Tay
And prosperity to Professor Cox who has given £30,000 upward and away

To help erect the bridge of the Tay
Near by Dundee and the Magdalen Green.

Beautiful railway bridge of the Silvery Tay
I hope that God will protect the passengers by night and by day
And that no accident will befall them while crossing the bridge of
the Silvery Tay
For that would be most awful to be seen
Near by Dundee and the Magdalen Green.

Beautiful railway bridge of the Silvery Tay
And prosperity to Messrs Bouche and Groat
The famous engineers of the present day
Who have succeeded erecting the railway bridge of the Silvery Tay
Which is unequal to be seen
Near by Dundee and the Magdalen Green.

My father was an ambitious man
'Hurry,' he'd say, 'Hurry and get a
literary reputation if you can'
So I wrote *Hamlet*
And was hailed by the nation
The first prize was Victoria
Station.

It was a pleasant region where, unheeded, I would commune with creatures of my fancy; I fancied elephants but there were none in Scotland. I wrote then in the most common-place style – 'Cor blimey Fred, ya got a big willy, s'truth.' I could not figure to myself that romantic woes or wonderful events would ever be my lot; but I was not confined to my own identity – I used to black up myself, beat a tom-tom and pretend to be a Zulu.

My husband, however, was from the first very anxious

that I should prove myself worthy of my parentage and enrol myself on the page of fame. He was forever inciting me to obtain a literary reputation. 'Hurry,' he'd say, 'Hurry and get a literary reputation and enrol yourself on the page of fame.'

We visited Switzerland and became neighbours of Lord Byron, who was writing the third canto of *Childe Harold*. By the time he had written the tenth canto of *Childe Harold*, the Childe was 35.

Some volumes of ghost stories, translated from the German into French, fell into our hands. Someone pushed them and we caught them. There was the *History of the Inconstant Lover*, who, when he thought to clasp the bride to whom he had pledged his vows, found himself in the arms of the pale ghost of her whom he had deserted. Then there was the tale of the sinful founder of his race, the Two Thousand Guineas: his gigantic, shadowy form was clothed, like the ghost in *Hamlet*, in complete armour, but with the beaver up it was very painful and could kruple his blurzon. He was to bestow the kiss of death on all the younger sons so, in his clanking armour, he advanced to the couch of the blooming youths who were cradled in healthy sleep. Eternal sorrow sat upon his face as he bent down and kissed the foreheads of the boys who [wait for it!] from that hour withered like the flowers snapped upon the stalk. But, alas, the cost of the funerals finally bankrupted him. He sold his suit of armour to raise money and the suit was crushed into a metal square and made into a Mini-Minor which was bought by a priest.

'We will each write a ghost story,' said Lord Byron. Poor Signor Polidori had some terrible idea about a skull-headed lady who was so punished for peeping through a keyhole, she saw what all keyhole peepers see – a couple screwing on the bed. He did not know what to do with her and was obliged to dispatch her to the tomb of the Capulets. Alas, when she got there they were both dead so she went for a coffee.

I busied myself *to think of a story*, a story that would curdle the blood of the reader and loosen the sphincter. Every ghost story must have a beginning. The Hindus gave the world an elephant to support it, but they make the elephant stand upon a tortoise. In practical terms the tortoise would have been crushed to a pulp. Perhaps that's what is wrong with the world – we are all living on a crushed tortoise.

Many and long were the conversations between Lord Byron and Shelley; some were eighteen feet tall. They talked to Dr Darwin and one of his experiments. He had preserved a piece of vermicelli in a glass case till by some extraordinary means it began to move with voluntary motion. Again, you could put some spaghetti in a glass case and wait for it to become animated, then you could let it go and it could then run free in the streets.

I did not sleep that night; my mind wandered. I saw a pale student of unhallowed arts kneeling beside the monster he had put together. I saw the hideous phantasm of a man stretched out and then, on the working with some powerful engine, he shows signs of life, sits up and says, 'Hello dar, what's de time?' Frightful must it be; for supremely frightful would be the effect of any human endeavour to mock the stupendous mechanism of the Creator of life – which as we all know is a flat tortoise.

So when the hitherto inanimate body sat up, opened his eyes and said, 'Hello dere, lend us a quid,' I opened my eyes in terror. The idea so possessed my mind that a thrill of fear ran through me and out the back.

Swift as light, and as cheering, was the idea that broke in upon me: 'I have found it! What terrified me will terrify others; and I need only describe the spectre which had haunted my midnight pillow.' On the morrow I announced that I had *thought of a story*.

At first I thought but a few pages – of a short tale, about 5 feet 3 inches, but Shelley urged me to develop the idea to a greater length, 100 feet 6 inches. I certainly did not owe the suggestion of any one incident to my husband. In fact, he did bugger all. However, but for his incitement it would never have taken form, and all he wanted was 60% of the royalties.

And now, once again, I bid my hideous progeny go forth and prosper. Open a tie shop! Its several pages speak of many a walk, many a drive, and many a takeaway curry.

I have changed no portion of this story.

M.W.S.
London, October 15th, 1831

PREFACE
(By P. B. Shelley, 1818)

This Preface has absolutely nothing to do with Mary's book. It is written so I'll have a few fingers in the pie when the book starts to sell.

VOLUME ONE

LETTER I

To Mrs Saville, England
St Petersburgh, Dec. 11th, 17—.

You will rejoice to hear that no disaster has accompanied the commencement of an enterprise which you regarded with such evil forebodings. I did not catch fire nor was I sucked down in a whirlpool or eaten by a polar bear. Perhaps these are the things you had in mind for me.

I am already far north of London and as I walk in the crap-ridden streets of Petersburgh I feel a cold northern breeze play on my cheeks, which braces my nerves and warms my swannicles. Do you understand these feelings? If not, feel yourself in bed tonight. I try in vain to be persuaded that the North Pole is the seat of God and his angels, tho they must wear warm clothes; it ever presents itself to my imagination as the region of beauty and delight and McDonald's. There, Margaret, the sun is very low in the sky, but if you go upstairs and stand on the chair you will be able to see it although, like my bank balance, it has almost disappeared. If only my bank balance would rise on the horizon every morning, oh how happy I would be. However, I have trust in the preceding navigators. We are preceded by about a dozen in a small boat. One claims to be Henry of Navarre. I think he's a bloody liar, his name is actually Dick Smith.

The snow and frost are banished and we are sailing over a calm sea. We may be wafted to a land surpassing in wonders and in beauty every region hitherto discovered on the habitable globe. There is the phenomena of the heavenly bodies. When I think of heavenly bodies I think of Doris Riter's body of 36 Roseland Road, Catford. What may not be expected in a country of eternal light? Well, for a start it never gets dark. I may have discovered the wondrous power which attracts the needle. I may go to parts of the world where no human eye has ever set foot. These are my enticements, to conquer all fear of danger or death. If the latter should happen, I will stop immediately. I feel the joy a young boy feels when he embarks in a little boat with his holiday mates on an expedition of discovery up a native river. If I remember correctly, that is how Livingston died.

I shall find the secret of the magnet and I will become admired far and wide [he speaks well of himself]. I feel an enthusiasm which elevates me to heaven, for nothing contributes so much to tranquillise the mind as does a steady purpose, or Valium. It is regret which I had felt as a child on learning that my father's injunction had forbidden my uncle to allow me to embark on a seafaring life. Fuck him, I'll do as I please.

> I must go down to the sea again
> To the lonely sea and the sky
> And all I ask is a tall ship
> And a star to steet her by.

One day my name will go down beside Drake's and Nelson's. In fact I believe some people can't wait for me to join them.

Six years have passed since I resolved on my present undertaking. (He was an undertaker as well as a sailor.) I remember how I prepared for this enterprise. I stripped naked and covered my body with bear's grease. I accompanied the whale-fishers on several expeditions to the North Sea, and several times I fell into it. I voluntarily endured cold, famine, thirst and want of sleep and did it all in the comfort of my hotel room because I just couldn't keep up with the sailors. I hired myself as a mate on a Greenland whaler and acquitted myself to the admiration of the crew, except that during the whole voyage I was violently seasick. I must own to feeling a little proud when the captain offered me a boat to row back home.

I'm now a fisherman
I strip naked and cover myself in
  bear's grease
I dive over the side, I nearly
  bloody freeze
I catch fish with my teeth
Alas, I foundered on a reef

Dear Margaret, I now deserve to accomplish some great purpose – become Admiral, Field Marshal or manager of Boots. My life has been passed in ease and luxury, and in being seasick. Oh, that some encouraging voice would answer in the affirmative.

This is the most favourable period for travelling in Russia. They fly quickly over the snow in their sledges. Some have difficulty stopping the horses which seem to go on and on and they are never seen again. The cold is not excessive if you are wrapped up in furs with an electric heater attached. It would need to be full on. The difficulty is carrying the heavy batteries under your arm. This is a dress which I have already adopted, but carrying the batteries has given me a hernia – this too is electrically heated. There is a great difference between walking the deck and remaining seated, motionless for hours. The latter people freeze to death and have to be thrown overboard. I have no ambition to be thrown overboard so I walk continuously, backwards and forwards, holding my heated hernia in place.

I shall depart from this town in a fortnight or three weeks; my intention is to hire a ship, which can be easily done by slipping the hawsers off when the owner is not looking.

Your affectionate brother,
R. Walton

We had a sto'way in the hold
He was an eccentric
millionaire we were told
Every night we'd throw him
over the side
He'd say 'thanks for the ride'
And the crew threw him
overboard on the next tide
Eventually he died.

LETTER II

To Mrs Saville, England.
Archangel, March 18th, 17—.

How slowly the time passes up here. Up here one hour takes three. Encompassed as I am by frost, snow and ice, yet I have hired a vessel. It is a very secure ship with a slight tendency to sink. Just in case, we all sleep in the lifeboats.

I have no friend, Margaret; I think this is because I have got halitosis. The men stand 50 yards away whenever they want to talk to me. I am glowing with the enthusiasm of success, but there will be none to participate in my joy. Still, I am wearing a furry hat and every evening I sing 'God Save the Queen' through the porthole. I know she can't hear me but there's no reason why I shouldn't.

I shall commit my thoughts to paper, or the wall or the floor or even the ceiling. But that is a poor medium for the communication of feeling. Talking of medium, we have one travelling with us in the steerage. He has a mystic power. He can give us the exact date and day every day. I desire the company of a man who could sympathise with me and his company must have a good annual turnover. I bitterly feel the want of a friend. (I have no one near me except the ship's cat.) Someone who has tastes like my own – chicken madras.

I am self-educated: for the first fourteen years of my life I ran wild on the common. At the end of that time I fell exhausted to the ground. By the time I was fifteen I had recovered from my fourteen-year run. At that age I became acquainted with poets of our own country: Goethe, Adolph Hitler, Goering. Now one becomes acquainted with more languages than that of my native country. Now I am twenty-eight, and am in reality more illiterate than many schoolboys of fifteen. I speak two languages – good and bad.

> We have a sailor on board who's
> gay
> No one knows what got him that
> way
> I asked him what made him one
> 'It's . . .,' he said, 'It's a lot of fun.'

Well, I will certainly find no friends on the wide ocean. Every day I scan the seas for one and I never see one person – perhaps he's inland.

The master is a person remarkable in the ship for his gentleness and mild of discipline. He likes to talk to young sailors with his hand on his hip. I cannot overcome an intense distaste to the usual brutality exercised on board ship. I have never believed it to be necessary to give a man 50 lashes, then keelhaul him, then hang him from the yard arm, then finally make him walk the plank or swallow an anchor. Very few sailors survive this ritual.

I am preparing to depart. I am going to unexplored regions, 'to the land of mist and snow'; but I shall kill no albatross, therefore do not be alarmed for my safety. If you see an albatross, he can be one I did not kill.

So, dear sister, continue to write to me by every opportunity and don't forget to enclose the postal orders.

Your affectionate brother,
Robert Walton

LETTER III

To Mrs Saville, England.
July 7th, 17—.

My dear Sister,

I write a few lines in haste to say that I am safe. My men are bold and apparently firm of purpose. But the floating sheets of ice that continually pass us, indicating the dangers of the region towards which we are advancing, appear to dismay them. They all shrink from their posts and huddle together in fear, many crossing themselves. Why not? They have crossed everybody else.

My swelling heart involuntarily pours itself out thus. The doctor says it's a vascular leak. But I must finish. Heaven bless my beloved sister.

R.W.

P.S. Please keep sending the postal orders.

LETTER IV

To Mrs Saville, England.
August 5th, 17—.

So strange an accident has happened to us. My seamen groaned. A strange sight attracted our attention. We perceived a low carriage, fixed on a sledge and drawn by dogs, pass on towards the north at the distance of half a mile but which had the shape of a man, apparently of gigantic stature. He was smoking a cigarette. He sat in the sledge and guided the dogs. We watched the rapid progress of the traveller with our telescopes until he was lost among the distant inequalities of the ice.

In the morning I went on deck and found all the sailors busy on one side of the vessel, apparently talking to someone in the sea. It was a sledge, like that we had seen before, which had drifted towards us in the night on a large fragment of ice. Only one dog remained alive; but there was a human being with it. He was not, as the other traveller seemed to be, a savage inhabitant. When I appeared on deck, the master said, 'Here is our captain, and he will not allow you to perish on the open sea. Come aboard and he will give you beans on toast and Horlicks.'

On perceiving me, the stranger addressed me in English, although with a foreign accent. 'Before I come on board,' said he, 'will you have the kindness to inform me whither you are bound.'

I replied that we were on a voyage of discovery, in search of heaven, and if he came aboard I would give him beans on toast and Horlicks.

Upon hearing this he came aboard. Good God! Margaret, if you had seen the man who thus capitulated for his safety . . . His limbs were frozen, and his body dreadfully emaciated by cold and fatigue; his penis had snapped off. I never saw a man in so wretched a condition. We attempted to carry him into the cabin, but as soon as he had quitted the fresh air he fainted! We accordingly brought him back to the deck, and restored him to animation by rubbing him with brandy and forcing him to swallow a small quantity. He forced himself to swallow quite a large quantity. As soon as he showed signs of life, we wrapped him up in blankets and placed him near the chimney of the kitchen stove. By slow degrees he recovered and ate at great speed some of the beans on toast. We had to stand clear of him.

Two days passed in this manner before we could get close enough to speak. Then, when my guest was a little recovered, I had trouble keeping off the men who wished to ask him a thousand questions – What's the Pope's inside leg measuirement? What's your blood group? Have you ever had prostate trouble? Do you like beans on toast and Horlicks? The lieutenant asked why he had come so far off the ice.

'To seek the one who fled from me.'

'And did the man who you pursued travel in the same fashion?'

'Yes.'

'Then I fancy we have seen him, for the day before we picked you up, we saw some dogs drawing a sledge, with a man in it, across the ice. He was huge, he would have knocked the shit out of you.'

This aroused the stranger. Alone with me he said, 'Thank you for having rescued me from a strange and perilous situation.'

'Oh it is nothing,' I said, 'we are only charging you for bed and breakfast.'

August 19th, 17—.

Dear Sister,

The stranger, whose name is Victor Frankenstein, is still travelling on the ship with me and his intellect is very satisfying; he speaks two languages – good and bad. He has told me that he will tell me his story and commence his narrative tomorrow when I am at leisure. Please keep sending the postal orders.

Yours,
Robert

My father was very attracted to children
from the hills
He found this blonde beauty, she was
called Jill
He adopted her and took her to Rome
Where she proceeded to eat them out of
house and bloody home.

CHAPTER I

I am by birth a Genevese. I was brought up by the Christian Brothers and I was brought down by Mrs Doris Munger of Lewisham. My ancestors had been for many years counsellors and syndics and my father had filled several public situations: (1) he was a lavatory attendant (2) he was a dustman and (3) a street sweeper, posts which he served with honour and reputation. He was respected by all who knew him. He passed his younger days perpetually occupied by affairs of his country. He had quite a few himself until he was caught.

A variety of circumstances had prevented his marrying early – he was ugly. It was not until the decline of life that he became a husband and the father of a family.

As the circumstances of his marriage illustrate his character, he married a nymphomaniac. One of his most intimate friends was a merchant from a flourishing state, who fell through numerous mischances – one was a coal hole. He had back trouble. People who borrowed money never gave it back. This man, whose name was Beaufort, and his great grandfather had invented the solid-lead violin for the deaf. He was of proud and unbending disposition and could not bear to live in poverty and oblivion in the same country where he had formerly been a distinguished dustman. Having paid his debts with cheques stamped RTD – his one heirloom – he took to wearing a diamond-studded jock strap. He had to retreat because he lived unknown and in wretchedness.

My father loved Beaufort with the truest friendship. He bitterly deplored the false pride which led his friend to a conduct so little worthy of the affection that united them. He lost no time in endeavouring to seek him out. He went round the streets with a stop watch, ringing a bell and shouting, 'Beaufort, for Christ's sake where are you man?'

Beaufort had taken effectual measures to conceal himself: he painted himself black and it was ten months before the paint wore off. My father discovered his abode and hastened to the house. But when he entered, misery and despair alone welcomed him. Beaufort had saved but a very small sum of money from the wreck of his fortunes but it was sufficient to provide him with sustenance, which was all he ate. He was so poor that he had the arse out of not his but somebody else's trousers. At length his grief took so fast hold of his mind that at the end of three months he lay on a bed of sickness, incapable of any exertion except to play the trombone.

Caroline Beaufort possessed a mind of an uncommon mould: it was back to front, but her courage rose to support her in her adversity. She procured plain work; she plaited straw blankets. She plaited a straw blanket for her father; she earned a sustenance.

Several months passed in this manner. Her father smoked and set fire to his straw blanket. Her father grew worse. Her time was entirely occupied in attending him and his trombone. Her means of subsistence decreased and in the tenth month her father died in her arms, leaving her an orphan and a beggar, a terrible inheritance. The orphan was adopted but they told the beggar to 'bugger off'. The last blow overcame her, and she knelt by Beaufort's coffin weeping. When my father entered the chamber it was flooded. He came like a protecting spirit to the poor girl and her magnificent bosom. After the interment of his friend he conducted her to Geneva, and placed her under the protection of a relation. Two years later, he shot his wife. Caroline and her magnificent boobs then became his wife.

They seemed to grow in their bonds of devoted affection. There was a sense of justice in my father's upright mind which rendered it necessary that he should approve highly in order to love strongly. He did it to her six times a day; then he would rest for a fortnight. During former years he had suffered from the late-discovered unworthiness of one beloved, and so was disposed to set a greater value on tried worth. He put a value of £100 on his beloved. Of course he did not know about the liaison between his wife and the milkman – he just wondered why they had not had a milk bill for a year. He strove to shelter her so, as a fair exotic is sheltered by the gardener from every rougher wind, he bought her an umbrella and he had a fence built round her to protect her. Her health and even the tranquillity of her hitherto constant spirit had been shaken by what she had gone through. She had gone through £10,000. During the two years that had elapsed previous to their marriage, my father had gradually relinquished all his public functions – railway guard, hotel porter and tallyman.

They travelled to Italy, they visited Germany, France and Bexhill-on-Sea. Their eldest child was born in

Naples. For several years I was the only child. Much as they were attached to each other (they were joined at the hip) they seemed to draw inexhaustible stores of affection from a very mine of love to bestow on me. Yes that was it – I was a plaything and when they got tired of that, their idol, and as a last resort, they used me as a child. During every hour of my infant life I received the lessons of patience (for this I was locked in a cupboard for an hour), charity (they made me give them all my pocket money) and, finally, karate lessons.

For a long time, apart from the rent, I was their only expense. Occasionally, to prove my progress I would fell my father with a karate chop to the neck.

My mother often used to visit the poor. I didn't understand – we were the poor. To my mother this was more than a duty. For her to act in her turn the guardian angel to the afflicted was a great act in itself, and she travelled the halls with it. One house she visited contained some neglected children. It spoke of penury in the worst shape. In fact, one of the children spoke, 'This is penury in its worst shape.' Among the children was a very thin girl, fair with hair the brightest gold colour. It seemed to set a crown of distinction on her head. She had blue eyes.

When my father returned from Milan he found in the hall of our villa a child fairer than a pictured cherub – a creature who seemed to shed radiance from her looks and whose form and motions were lighter than the chamois of the hills. And, above all, she had good drainage. It would be unfair to keep her in poverty when we could give her a better quality of poverty. Her name was Elizabeth. Everyone loved her, even Lord Palmerston and Lord Nelson; everyone had the most reverential attachment, which was attached to her side. On the morning her parents presented Elizabeth to me as a promised gift, she arrived gift wrapped.

CHAPTER II

We were brought up together, only one inch separated us. I was capable of a more intense application and was deeply smitten with a thirst for knowledge. I got her to play doctors and nurses. At heart I was a dirty little devil. She busied herself with following the aerial creations of the poets. 'The nightingale. Blessed bard death wasn't meant for thee.' Now let some other bloody bird snuff it. It was summer, the brilliant sun, the flowers and cow pats, and Elizabeth pursued the world of nature. What causes elephants? I had never had them so I couldn't answer her.

On the birth of a second son, my parents gave up their wandering life and fixed themselves in their native country using contact glue. We possessed a villa in Venice. When we visited there I forgot and as I opened the back door I stepped straight into the canal. My parents' lives had passed into considerable seclusion. He locked himself in the loo all day and she locked herself in the attic all night. I united myself in the bonds of a close friend; he had a hundred pounds' worth. Henry Clerval was a boy of singular talents. He could play hop-scotch, and above all he liked whipping. He read books of chivalry, romance and Sade and he composed heroic songs: 'I've got a heroic bunch of coconuts, see them all standing in a row, big ones, little ones, ones as big as your head, etc., etc.' He liked characters – King Arthur and his Round Table, the one he had breakfast on. He wanted to shed blood to redeem the Holy Sepulchre from the Infidels which meant Saladin, who beat the shit out of the Crusaders.

Saladin was fighting for Jerusalem
He said the city belonged to him
He and his calvary charged the
city
But they missed, 'twas such a pity.

My parents were possessed by a generous spirit, usually 90% proof Famous Grouse.

My temper was sometimes violent and I was given to swinging a cat round and round my head in a room just to prove there was enough space to swing one. I was trying to solve the physical secrets of the world: did Queen Victoria have thin legs? and did John Brown wear anything under the kilt?

Clerval was desperate to be a horse in the charge of the Light Brigade. To this effect he went around wearing a saddle on his back and charging imaginary Russian guns.

I had exquisite pleasure in dwelling on the recollections of my childhood – a bottle, my potty, and my crap-filled nappy.

One day we went to the baths near Thonon. The inclement weather obliged us to remain a day, confined to the inn. I chanced to find a volume of the works of Cornelius Agrippa. I opened it; a new light seemed to dawn upon my mind. I communicated my discovery to my father who said, 'Ah, Cornelius Agrippa. My dear Victor, do not waste your time upon this crap.' Apparently, Agrippa's theories were crap and had been entirely exploded – which blew his leg off.

I found Cornelius Agrippa's book
I thought I'd have a look
He opened up my mind
He did it from behind
I've still got the scar
Which can be seen from afar.

When I returned home my first care was to procure what works were left of this author. They consisted of a wooden leg and Paracelsus and Albetus Magnus. I read and studied the wild fancies of these writers – most of them fancied women with big tits. I always came from my studies discontented and unsatisfied. Sir Isaac Newton said he felt like a child picking up shells beside the ocean but never finding one. So? I had gazed upon the fortifications and impediments that seemed to keep human beings from entering the citadel of nature, and rashly and ignorantly I had repined. [This is a lot of bollocks. Ed.]

So once a year
Scientists went 100 feet down in a
sphere
They ran out of air
So they got out of there

One tried holding his breath
This brought on his death.

But here were books and here were men who had penetrated deeper and knew no more. Some had descended to a depth of 300 fathoms but couldn't hold their breath any longer and had to ascend having proved bugger all. I was self-taught with regard to my favourite studies; hunchbacks and fairies. My father was not scientific but he could juggle with melons. I entered, with the greatest diligence, into the subject of the philosopher's stone and where he had hidden it, and the elixir of life. The nearest thing that man had to that was Horlicks. Some disbelieved in Horlicks as the elixir of life and said it actually was Oxo. Wealth was an inferior object, but by God it paid the rent. But the glory would attend to the discovery if I could find ways to make man invulnerable to any violent death, like an elephant falling on him.

Then there was the raising of ghosts and devils. If my incantations were always unsuccessful, people would point me out in the street and say, 'See him, his incantations are unsuccessful.' I attributed my failure to wearing skin-tight underpants to avoid ants getting in. And thus for a time I was occupied by exploded systems. There were dozens of explosions going on throughout the house. One blew up my father's breakfast, another one blew him up. One explosion blew my mother off the W.C. at a critical moment.

One day there was a violent and terrible thunderstorm that burst at once with frightful loudness and ripped my trousers off. I remained while the storm lasted, watching its progress. I beheld a stream of fire issue from an old and beautiful oak. It stood just a few yards from where I stood and my face was smoke-blackened. My mother screamed when she saw me. 'Help,' she shouted, 'There's a nigger in the house with no trousers on!'

I at once gave up my former occupations – clog dancing, bare-back riding and pheasant plucking. I set down natural history and all its progeny as a deformed and abortive creation, i.e., a three-legged cripple. Are we bound to prosperity or ruin? When I look back it seems to me that this remarkable change of inclination and will was a suggestion of the guardian angel of my life – Dick Tonk. [What in God's name is he talking about? Ed.]

CHAPTER III

When I was seventeen and had learned to spell cat, dog and duck, they decided I should become a student at the university of Ingolstadt. I should be made acquainted with the customs of my country, with dwarf hurling, haddock stretching and ostrich strangling. My sister had caught scarlet fever, and she caught it with a butterfly net. During her illness we had to prevent my mother nursing her to death. Elizabeth was saved, but the consequence of this imprudence was fatal. On the third day, mother sickened; but for this illness she would be back home boiling custard. Even on her death bed her fortitude continued – she did 250 press ups; it proved too much for her and she died. 'It is all our bloody daughter's fault,' said father.

> I went to my mother's funeral
> It was raining with a grey sky
> But in her coffin, she was nice and
>   dry
> I wanted to cry, but I could only
>   try, try, try.

I need not describe the feelings of those whose dearest ties were with the Lords Taverners, Grenadier Guards, and the Royal Artillery. During the Napoleonic wars my father had volunteered to serve with Lord Nelson's cricket team. Nelson bowled him with his good arm for a duck. They were playing on deck during the battle and a Spanish marksman, knowing nothing of cricket, shot Nelson and play was halted for the day.

The funeral over, I departed for Ingolstadt. I desired to see my Elizabeth consoled. She indeed veiled her grief – she put a blanket over her head and looked through a hole. I left her to her life or ironing, cooking, mountain climbing, scuba diving and dwarf hurling.

On the day of my departure, Clerval spent the evening balancing on one leg and sword swallowing. Henry felt the misfortune of being debarred from a life of idleness and financial ruin.

Next morning, grabbing the seat of my trousers, I threw myself into the chaise and shot out the other side. I love my brother Edward and my friend Clerval. Such were my reflections, which I managed by bending down and observing myself in the seat of my shiny trousers.

There came into my life a Mr Krempe. He was uncouth – he used to be couth, but he forgot. He asked me several questions, the first was 'lend us a quid?'

He said, 'Have you really spent your time studying that crap?'

I replied, 'I have studied that crap, what crap did you study?'

'I studied a different crap in Ancient Greek.'

So saying, he stepped aside and into it. He sold me several books, charging £1.00 a time. By the time he had finished, I had a pile of books and he was a millionaire.

Mr Krempe had huge ears which looked like people looking over his shoulders.

As a child I had not been content with the results promised by a philosopher of natural science. One such promise was that by waving my arms I should be able to fly. I proved that to be a myth, so I blew his brains out. I realised that Kant, Hegel and Freud were all cunts. I had utter contempt for these three mentioned Charlies. They all sought immortality but in the end they all snuffed it. I was required to exchange chimeras of boundless grandeur for realities of little worth. I exchanged my chimera ten times a day and ended up with fuck all.

I thought of Mr Krempe and recalled what he had said of Mr Waldman.

I went into the lecturing room. Mr Waldman entered shortly after. He appeared about fifty and disappeared about seventy. He was a redhead; no hair, just a red head. He was short for his height – three feet two inches. He began his lecture by singing 'Ave Maria'. After a few preparatory experiments, he concluded with 'A good big un will always beat a good little un.' To prove it, I knocked him down.

Mr Waldman lectured on Ave
  Maria
He knew her dimension from ear
  to ear
Her blood group was 'A'
She used it every day
'It's,' she said, 'the best way'
Alas, that night she passed away.

Modern masters promise very little; they know that metals cannot be transmuted and that the elixir of life is a chimera on sale at all good chimeraists. Scientists penetrate nature and show how she works in her hiding-places – usually Bradford. And on the third day they rise again from the dead, ascend into heaven and sit at the right hand of God the Father Almighty. They have discovered how the blood circulates (through the veins, would you believe it?) and the nature of the air we breathe (it's invisible and full of crap). They can command the thunders of heaven, mimic the earthquake and even do Al Jolson. Something was wrong. I didn't come to this school to be destroyed. If I am, they should lower the fees. I will pioneer a new way, explore unknown powers, and unfold to the world the deepest mysteries of creation. This was going to get me right in the shit.

I closed not my eyes that night, only the doors. My internal being was in a turmoil – I had to swallow an enema. I believed myself to possess a natural talent, that was making moustard.[1] I visited Waldman. I listened to his statement that was delivered without any presumption, except for a burst on the banjo. He said how ignorant they were and how enlightened were those who had removed prejudices against modern chemists like Boots.

'I am happy,' said Mr Waldman, 'to have gained a disciple. Chemistry has had a great many improvements. They now have suppositories for piles and are able to take the temperature of boiling water and the temperature of a monkey with malaria.' So I set out to take the temperature of boilding water and searched for a monkey with malaria so that I might take his temperature. Anything to forward my studies.

[1]Unexplainable.

Winter, Spring and Summer passed
away
So did Queen Vic they say
She died with a bad heart
The damn thing wouldn't start
It meant nothing to me
I was looking for bits for my monster you
see.

CHAPTER IV

From this day, chemistry in the most comprehensive sense became my sole occupation. Every day I would boil a vat of water and take its temperature and then the monkey with malaria had his temperature taken. So it went on.

Krempe had a great deal of sound sense but he had a repulsive physiognomy. He had a face like a dog's bum and the dirty devil let off in confined spaces. Professor Krempe often asked me, with a sly smile, how Cornelius Agrippa went on? I said that he went on the bus. At the same time Mr Waldman expressed the most heartfelt exultation in my progress: 'I have the most heartfelt exultation in your progress,' he said. Two years passed, during which time I paid no visit to Geneva but was engaged heart and soul in pursuit of some discoveries through which I hoped to make a monster. None but those who have experienced them can conceive of the enticements of science – one is money. In other studies you go as far as others have gone before you. Some got as far as Bexhill-on-Sea, which is not a seat of learning. In scientific pursuit there is continual food for discovery; I had discovered sausage and mash with mushy peas. I, who continually sought the attainment of one object: sausage and chips and mushy peas.

One of the phenomena which had peculiarly attracted my attention was the structure of the human frame. I discovered it was made up mostly of bones, skin and veins, all of which could be made into a nourishing soup. Then I asked myself, how did the principle of life proceed? The answer was mostly on foot. Next, how would life proceed to be a mystery? To find out, I shot somebody and waited by the corpse. Finally, I took it to the morgue. In life he had been a butcher. I sat by the body all night with some cheese sandwiches and a thermos of Horlicks. In the morning the sandwiches and Horlicks were gone but he was still there and still as stiff. The moral of this story was, if you shoot a butcher, he stops working. Suddenly in the midst of this darkness a light broke in upon me, a light so brilliant it must have been 200 watts, while I became dizzy with the immensity of the prospect which it illustrated. I was surprised that among so many men of genius, like George Formby, I alone should be reserved to discover so astounding a secret.

Remember, I am *not* recording the vision of a madman. I have succeeded in discovering the cause of generation of life. I became capable of bestowing animation upon lifeless matter, like I could make a doormat shake itself and I could make a couch animate and run around the room. I could boil an egg just by looking at it. What had been the study and desire of the wisest men since the creation of the world was now within my grasp, i.e., life. I was like the Arabian who had been buried with the dead and who found a passage to life, aided only by one glimmering and seemingly ineffectual light that led me to the Stock Exchange where I met Jeffrey Archer who immediately absconded with my life savings.

When I found so astonishing a power placed within my hands, I put it in my pocket. It was with these feelings I began the creation of a human being, but the size of his parts formed a great hindrance. I decided to make the being of a gigantic stature, about eight feet in height. I plundered the mortuary for parts and what I couldn't find I would take from the butcher's shop.

Life and death appeared to me to be ideal bounds, and most people are either one or the other. I could dig up the dead departed and put them on the lawn of the grieving and say to them, 'Give me four hundred guineas and I can bring that stiff back to life.' No man could refuse such an offer. This I did successfully for a few weeks.

My cheek had grown pale with study, and my person had become emaciated with confinement. Who could conceive the horrors of my dabbling among the unhallowed damps of the grave? But then a resistless and almost frantic impulse urged me forward – so I collided with a tree. I seemed to have lost all soul or sensation but for this one pursuit. It was indeed but a passing trance; it passed me at thirty miles per hour and disappeared. I returned to my old habits. I collected bones from charnel houses. They disturbed the tremendous secrets of the human frame. In a solitary chamber, or rather a cell, at the top of the house separated from all other apartments I kept my workshop of filthy creation; my eyeballs were starting from their sockets in attending to the details of my employment. The dissecting room and the slaughter-house furnished a pair of balls and a willy the right size for my monster. I stuck them on with glue, they looked marvellous. I knew my silence disquieted some of my friends. One of them said, 'Your silence disquiets me.'

I knew well how my father felt – it was usually my mother. My father made no reproach in his letters and only took notice of my silence by enquiring, 'What the fuck are you doing? Love, Dad.' Winter, spring and summer passed away. So did Queen Victoria. I did not watch the blossom or the expanding leaves; no, I was looking for bones and spare kidneys to fit an eight feet giant. I appeared to people like one doomed by slavery to toil in the ruins, or any other unwholesome trade like a pheasant plucker. Every night I was oppressed by a slow fever; it took two days to reach me. My monster was completed and all I had to do now was to give him the gift of life. The creature lay on a slab naked; he could not be allowed thus into society. I struggled with the lifeless body and put on him a pair of giant-sized trousers and a flannel shirt.

The monster's trousers fell to the floor
Some of it out the front
Round the back there was more
Underpants must be found
Before it spreads around.

The first words the monster spoke
'Has anyone got a smoke?
I'd give anything for a drag
On a fag.'

CHAPTER V

How can I describe my emotions at this catastrophe, or how delineate the wretch whom, with such infinite pains and care, I had endeavoured to form? There was the bolt that affixed his neck to his spine, there were the screws holding his forehead to his skull; but now was the moment of truth. I plunged the electrodes into his rectum and switched on the current. He gave a groan and he was alive! He spoke as he sat up, 'Have you got a fag mate?' My God, I had given birth to a nicotine junky! I handed him the cigarette which I lit then, leaping off the table, he stood there. But, alas, we had forgotten one thing: he had no support for his trousers which fell to the floor revealing his manhood in all its glory. If any women saw this they would be leaving their husbands in thousands. Quickly I got some string round his trousers. What had I done? No mortal could support the horror of that countenance! I rushed downstairs to the refuge of a cupboard where I remained during the rest of the night walking up and down in great agitation – something difficult to do in a cupboard.

I passed the night wretchedly sleeping on a clothes line. I sank to the ground through languor and extreme weakness and the doctor came and said, 'You have sunk to the ground through languor and extreme weakness.'

I continued walking in a depressed manner. I traversed the streets without any clear conception of where I was or what he was doing. He wasn't doing anything. My heart palpitated in the sickness of fear and I hurried on with irregular steps, not daring to look about me.

> Ohhhh . . . .
> Like one, on a lonesome road who,
> Doth walk in fear and dread,
> And, having once turned round,
> walks on,
> And turns no more his head;
> Because he knows a frightful fiend
> Doth close behind him tread.[2]

My eyes fixed on a coach that was coming towards me. It stopped just where I was standing. The door being opened, I perceived Henry Clerval, who sprang out of the coach and trod straight in it. 'My dear Frankenstein,' he exclaimed, 'how glad I am to see you!'

Clerval's presence brought back thoughts of my father, Elizabeth, and all those bloody hangers-on at home. I grasped his hand and the 100 kroner note in it. 'It gives me the greatest delight to see you but tell me how you left my father, my brothers and Elizabeth.'

'Penniless,' he replied. 'But my dear Frankenstein,' he continued, 'I did not before remark how very ill you appear, so thin and pale, you look as if you have been wanking for several nights.'

[2]Coleridge's *Ancient Mariner*.

We ascended into my room and, once seated, I was unable to contain myself. I was unable to remain for a single instant in the same place: I jumped over the chairs and climbed on top of the cupboard; I crawled under the table; I jumped out the window and ran back up the stairs and hid under the bed.

> I was very ill and what was wrong
>   with me was affecting my mind
> But the pain was coming from my
>   behind
> Perhaps the illness is in my bum
> It's amazing where illness can
>   come from.

'Victor, Victor,' cried Clerval, 'what the fuck's the matter with you?'

'Oh, save me! save me!' I imagined that the monster seized me; I struggled furiously and fell off the washing in a fit.

Clerval took the opportunity to put a straitjacket on me. I was lifeless and did not recover my sense for a long time – eighteen months.

I was very ill; I had no idea what the fuck was the matter with me but I raved incessantly about the monster. Doubtless my words suprised Henry. It persuaded him that my disorder indeed owed its origin to some uncommon and terrible event. He did not know what the fuck was the matter with me.

By very slow degrees, and some frequent relapses that alarmed and grieved my friend, they would tighten the straps on my straitjacket. All the while there was this twittering in my head. One day the gloom disappeared, but just in case they kept my straitjacket on. But what the fuck had been wrong with me?

'Dearest Clerval,' I exclaimed, 'the whole winter, instead of being spent studying as you promised yourself, you have been consumed with me and you have watched me being sick in my room. How shall I ever repay you?'

'A thousand guilders wouldn't go amiss,' said Clerval. 'You will repay me entirely, if you do not discompose yourself. May I speak to you of one subject? Compose yourself.'

Immediately I knocked off a 24 bar nocturne.

'I have observed your change of colour,' said Clerval.

I had gone a pale green.

> 'You're the strangest colour I've
>   ever seen
> You've gone dark green'
> So said my friend Clerval who
>   himself was ill in bed
> Going a bright colour red.

'Your father and cousin would be happy if they received a letter in your own handwriting.'

Immediately I wrote the letter 'A' and posted it to them.

'If this is your present temper, my friend, you will perhaps be glad to see a letter that has been lying here some days from you – to your cousin, I believe.'

CHAPTER VI

Frankenstein to Elizabeth:

Dearest Cousin,
Do not come here! The countryside abounds with wolves, bears and bandits!

Elizabeth to Frankenstein:

Clerval writes that indeed you are getting better and have stopped hiding in the cupboard. How pleased you would be to remark the improvement of our Ernest! He is now sixteen and full of activity and learning to yodel. He is not pleased with the idea of a military career overseas, playing bagpipes to the Scots Guards. In the meantime he is spending time in the open air, slapping his thighs and yodelling.

My dearest aunt and cousin died. We buried them; it seemed the best thing to do. The mortician did a job lot – he buried them all together. She, my aunt, was a Roman Catholic and she had pieces of the true cross. Put all of the pieces of the true cross together and it would show that Jesus was sixty feet high and eighty feet across. Poor girl, Justine; she wept and we were up to our ankles in tears.

Elizabeth Lavenza
Geneva, March 18th, 17—.

Frankenstein to Elizabeth:

Dear Elizabeth,

You say one word would suffice to quiet your fears. Here it is – C O L O U R! You can choose whatever you like – white, black, red, brown, blue, Russian blue, yellow, ochre. Yes, the word can go a long way.

One of my first duties on my recovery was to introduce Clerval to several professors. I introduced him to several Professor Waldman. In the absence of the other several professors, he will do. They have taken everything out of my laboratory – several noses, sets of false teeth, twelve legs, six vials of blood, twelve feet of veins, some spare kidneys, and a bottle of tomato sauce, etc. They were charging me 10 Marks a minute rent so I had to rush in, stay for three minutes, and rush out again. It was the only way I could afford it.

I writhed under Professor Waldman's words of praise but dared not exhibit the pain I felt. Clerval curled up on the floor in front of me, his legs behind his head, and said, 'This puts me in a very difficult position.' My sin in the back of my mind was that of a monster with his trousers down.

Mr Krempe was quite docile – I kept him on a lead. He was given to bursts of speech. 'Damn the fellow,' cried he. 'Why Mr Clerval has outstripped us all. He's a youngster who but a few years ago believed in Cornelius Agrippa, the Gem, the *Hotspur* and *Boys' Own*.'

Mr Krempe now commenced to eulogise. He did it in a bush. Clerval had never sympathised with my tastes for natural science. He came to university to master the Oriental languages.

The Persian, Arabic and Sanskrit – what a waste! No one in Switzerland spoke them and for the rest of his life he would have to talk to himself in one of these three languages. There were only three works of the Orientalists: the Omar Khayyám Ice Cream Factory, the King Durius Sewage Works and the Sheik Hussein Laundry.

Summer passed away, having been delayed by several accidents: (1) I was run over by a train; (2) I fell over a cliff and (3) I fell down a well. The roads were deemed impassable with snow.

During the month of May I expected the letter daily which was to fix the date of my departure. As I was still down a well I found it very hard to answer. Henry proposed a pedestrian tour in the environs of Ingolstadt and I acceded with pleasure to this proposition: I was fond of exercise but not that bloody fond. In the end it was to prove too strenuous for me. My health deteriorated; I tried very hard. I was taken for the salubrious air of the Alps but when I breathed it I fainted. In a few days I recovered.

Henry rejoiced in my gaiety and I started to yodel. He exerted himself to amuse me: he would juggle three bags of flour, he stood on his head and yodelled the 'William Tell Overture', he played the banjo and danced. He could make himself disappear; this he did by the simple expedient of leaving the room. His conversation was full of imagination. He spoke in Persian and Arabic; that was wonderful, but I didn't understand a bloody word. He repeated my favourite Wordsworth poem:

> I wandered lonely as a cloud
> That drifts aloft over dales and
> hills

And all at once I came upon
My dog being sick on the daffodils.

Clerval believed the world was flat, but he kept tripping over it.

We returned to our college on a Sunday afternoon: the peasants were dancing and hurling each other off cliffs into the lake. It was an old custom and they never tired of it, except those who drowned. My own spirits were high and I bounded along with feelings of unbridled joy and hilarity. From a great distance my family could see me bounding with unbridled joy and hilarity.

CHAPTER VII

On my return I found the following letter from my father:

My dear son,

You expect a happy and glad welcome and a box of gift-wrapped suppositories for your haemorrhoids. Well fuck your luck. But how can I relate our misfortune? William is dead! – di diddly I di – dead; he has stopped yodelling. One day he went for a walk but did not return. We searched for him until night fell and then we returned to the house. About five in the morning I discovered my lovely boy, who the night before I had seen blooming and yodelling, stretched on the grass lifeless and motionless. He was as stiff as a poker. His neck had been broken and his face was facing backwards. In other words he was lying face downwards on his back. He was conveyed home in a wheelbarrow. The anguish visible on my countenance betrayed the secret to Elizabeth. The fact that the body was rigid was another giveaway. She was very keen to see the corpse; she likes that sort of thing. Seeing the corpse, she fainted away; a bucket of water soon revived her. The previous day William had teased her to let him wear a very valuable miniature. It was an ivory elephant and he wanted to use it as fishing bait.

Come, Victor, not brooding thoughts of vengeance against the assassin – but just in case would you bring a musket, a sword, a brace of pistols and a bomb.

Your affectionate and afflicted father,
Alphonse Frankenstein
Geneva, May 12th, 17—.

'My dear Frankenstein,' exclaimed Henry, when he perceived me weeping with bitterness, 'are we always to see you unhappy, you miserable bastard?'

I motioned him to take up the letter so he took it up to the first floor while I walked up and down the room from north to south, to east and west, to nor-noreast, to sou-souwest, to 20° west, to 30° east – by which time I had covered the whole room.

'I can offer you no consolation,' said he.

'Then piss off,' said I.

'Now I go instantly to Geneva: come with me, Henry, to order four horses over the counter.' I held up four fingers to make sure we got them. As soon as the horses arrived I hurried into a cabriolet and bade farewell to my friend.

My journey was very uncomfortable as I was suffering from piles and looking forward to the gift of suppositories. I wished to hurry home for I longed to console and sympathise with the miserable bloody lot back home.

As I approached my home
I recognised the dome
I recognised the bailiff's men
Bringing out the furniture now
and then

The last contents they brought was
my mother
And then my invalid brother.

I remained two days at Lausanne in a painful state of mind and arse and then continued my journey towards Geneva. The road ran by the side of the lake which became narrower and narrower and narrower and finally it disappeared, and so did I; it took a month to find me again. As I approached my native town I discovered more distinctly the black sides of Jura and the bright summit of Mont Blancmange. I wept like a child – boo hoo hoo. 'Dear mountains! My own beautiful lake! How do you welcome your wanderer?' At that moment a landslide pushed me and the carriage into the lake. That's how they welcome their wandering kith and kin.

'Which are you,' said a peasant digging me out, 'are you kith or kin?'

'I am kith.'

'Well good, we don't want any kins here.'

Yet as I drew nearer home, grief and fear again overcame me so I did not care a fuck for the Jura or Mont Blancmange. Night also closed around and I could hardly see the dark mountains. My landlady said she had put a po under my bed but if I used it I was not to put it back under the bed because the steam rusts the springs.

As I cowered on deck it started to
rain
And, terrible luck, I fell in the lake
again

William, this storm is your funeral
hymn
But I got no bloody response from
him.

As I was unable to rest I resolved to visit the spot where my poor William had been murdered. As I could not pass through the town I was obliged to cross the lake in a boat to arrive at Plainpalais. During this short voyage, as I was rowing, the boat flooded and sank and I had to swim for the shore. I saw the lightning playing on the summit of Mont Blancmange. Already soaked to the skin, it started to rain again, absolutely flooding me. It was pitch dark until my eyes recovered themselves to the darkness. During that time I fell in the lake for a second time.

From the bank I watched the tempest, so beautiful yet terrific. This noble war in the sky elevated my spirits; I clasped my hands and exclaimed aloud: 'William, dear angel! this is thy funeral dirge.' [I don't think William heard it but it was well meant. Ed.] A flash of lightning illuminated the object and discovered its shape plainly to me, its gigantic stature. His trousers were still around his ankles. Each flash of lightning lit up his huge wedding tackle. What did he there? I waited, but he did nothing there. Was he the murderer of my brother? He suddenly rushed towards me. 'Have you got a fag?' he said. I hastily gave him a packet. Yes, he was the murderer! [There is not a shred of evidence against this poor monster. Ed.] Yes, it must have been two years since I gave this monster life. Was this his first crime? A murderer two years old? No court would believe it!

My first thought was to discover what I knew of the

murderer and cause instant pursuit to be made. 'Quick, police, fire, ambulance!' This being I had myself formed and given life to and met me at midnight. He asked me for a cheese sandwich. I told him I had no cheese, would fish paste do?

'Oh,' he queried, 'what will fish paste do?'

'Nothing,' I said, 'it just stays there.'

He asked me to help secure his trousers which I did, fixing them from the back where it was less dangerous.

It was about five in the morning when I entered my father's house. I told the servants not to disturb the family and they didn't but they, too, were still in bed. Six years had elapsed. I embraced my father, beloved parent. I gazed on the picture of my mother which stood over the mantelpiece. It was an historic subject painted at my father's desire and represented Caroline Beaufort in an agony of despair, kneeling by the coffin of her dead father. My father was really bent. Her garb was rustic and her cheek pale; but there was an air of dignity and beauty that hardly permitted the sentiment of pity. Nevertheless it was a bloody miserable painting. Below this picture was a miniature of William; my tears flowed when I looked upon it and soon the room was ankle deep in tears.

While I was thus engaged, Ernest entered. 'Still bloody miserable? Welcome home my dearest Dick,' he said.

'I'm not Dick,' said I, 'I'm Victor.'

'Poor William, he was our darling. We tried to revive him, we even tried a vet.'

Tears unrestrained – strained tears are much purer but less plentiful – fell from my brother's eyes. 'Elizabeth, alas, announced herself as having caused the death of William and that made her very wretched, but since the murderer has been discovered . . .'

Good God! How can that be? Who could attempt to pursue him? It is impossible; one might as well try to overtake the winds or confine a mountain stream with a straw. He disappeared at a speed of 100 miles per hour. He was eating a fish paste sandwich and his trousers kept falling down. The police, ambulance and fire brigade chased but he outstripped them.

'Indeed, who would credit that Justine Moritz became capable of so appalling a crime? The morning of the murder, servants had discovered in her pocket the ivory elephant brooch. She has been apprehended and charged with the murder.'

Nonsense! I knew that the murderer had been eating a fish paste sandwich and travelling at 100 miles per hour with his trousers down.

The real murderer was eating a
  sandwich of fish paste
To finish it he would have to make
  haste
His trousers were laying in haste
  on the floor
Could he ask for anything more?

My dear father, you are mistaken. Justine is innocent. No sir, I tried it on with her and she wasn't having any of it. I sincerely hope she will be acquitted. The murderer was a man with his trousers down, eating a fish paste sandwich and travelling at 100 miles per hour.

My tale was not one to announce publicly. I would tell it to someone privately in a cupboard.

We were soon joined by Elizabeth. Time had altered her since I last beheld her; it had endowed her with loveliness surpassing the beauty of her childish years – and huge boobs. She welcomed me with the greatest affection, and I gave them a quick squeeze.

'She is innocent, my Elizabeth,' said I.

'Yes, I too am innocent,' said Elizabeth.

'And me,' said father. 'And we are all of us innocent. Does that make you feel better?'

'Dearest niece,' said my innocent father, 'dry your tears. If she is Justine, as you believe, she will have to rely on the justice of our laws.'

'I tell you,' I said, 'that murderer had his trousers down, was eating fish paste sandwiches and travelling 100 miles per hour.'

'Of course he was,' said my father, helping me on with my straitjacket.

She related the evening of the night of the
sailor
I think he was a sailor or it might have
been a tailor
'All night I watched him go up and
down on my bed
By dawn he fell off dead.'

CHAPTER VIII

At Justine's court appearance I called out to the court from the witness box, declaring that she was innocent, that the murderer was eight feet tall, with his trousers down, travelling at 100 miles per hour and eating a fish paste sandwich. She entered the court, threw her eyes around the room and then caught them coming back.

She had been out the whole night with a sailor; the murder had been committed towards morning. A woman asked her what she did and she said, 'I did the sailor.' When another one enquired where she had passed the night she replied, 'With a sailor.'

A murmur of indignation and disbelief filled the court and the street. As the trial proceeded her countenance altered. One minute she was Tommy Cooper, then Lon Chaney, then Jimmy Durante and, finally, Frank Bruno. She collected her powers, then spoke in an audible although variable voice: she did Tom Jones, Frank Sinatra and Paul McCartney.

She related the evening of the night of the murder. She had been at the house of an aunt at Chêne with a sailor. On her return she met a sailor who asked her 'Would you like a fuck dear?' All through the night she watched him go up and down. As dawn broke she awoke and the sailor rolled off her, dead. From the back of the court I called out, 'It was a giant with his trousers down, eating a fish paste sandwich and travelling at 100 miles per hour.' That is all I said and for saying it they put me back in a straitjacket.

Several witnesses were called who said they had known her for many years. Many spoke well of her but were unwilling to come forward, so they went backwards and disappeared out of the court. During her service with us she was the most benevolent of human creatures. In her last illness she nursed Madam Frankenstein until it killed her. But public indignation had returned with renewed violence against her, with blackest ingratitude.

I perceived the countenances of the judges and they had already condemned my unhappy victim. I rushed out of the court in agony and was run over by a bus. I felt I had never before experienced such sensations of horror – not since I saw *Don't Forget Your Tooth Brush.* Words cannot convey an idea, only things like fork, hippo, nut cutlet, couch, tree, but none of them convey the heart-sickening despair.

'Yes,' said Elizabeth, 'we will go and visit her in jail and you, Victor, shall accompany me.' ('Oh fuck.') 'I cannot go alone.'

The idea of this visit was torture to me, yet I could not refuse. I didn't want to be seen going so I put a towel over my face. We entered the gloomy prison chamber and beheld Justine sitting on some straw at the far end; her hands were manacled and, with difficulty, she was trying to eat a packet of Smith's crisps. She rose on seeing us and threw herself at the feet of Elizabeth, weeping bitterly. We were soon all ankle deep in tears.

'Rise, my poor girl,' said Elizabeth. The poor girl rose six feet in the air and remained there.

'Would you like a sailor to make your last hours happy?'

'Can I come down now?' Justine asked. 'The local priest said that unless I gave £10 towards the church I will go to hell.'

'Then pay the £10 and avoid going to hell,' said Elizabeth.

'Dearest William, dearest blessed child! I soon shall be able to see you again, in heaven where we shall all be happy and I can see the strangle marks on your neck. Goodbye cruel world, goodbye. I leave a sad and bitter world, and that stupid man in the corner with the towel over his head.'

During this conversation I had retired to the corner of the prison room where I could conceal the horrid anguish that possessed me with a large piece of cardboard.

'I feel as if I could die in peace.' We all waited while she tried to die in peace but nothing happened.

Thus, the poor sufferer tried to comfort others – she tried to comfort the Pope, but before she could she would be strung up.

We stayed several hours with Justine and I danced with her three times.

On the morrow, Justine died, a favourite with Her Majesty's Royal Navy. I turned to contemplate the deep and voiceless grief of my Elizabeth but she wasn't there. All that woe and the desolation in the home. All was the work of my thrice-accursed hands, bloody hands multiplied by three. Justine's funeral was accompanied by wailing and lamentations and weeping. It was so bloody noisy we couldn't hear the coffin go into the ground.

Meanwhile, this monster was walking the countryside at 100 miles per hour, demanding cigarettes and strangling people if they did not give him one.

VOLUME TWO

CHAPTER I

I could never watch *Drop the Dead Donkey*; I could only watch it fall and pray for its soul. They say all the souls of dead donkeys go to Bexhill-on-Sea.

'Victor,' said my father, 'for fuck's sake snap out of it. I loved your brother.'

Tears came into his eyes; they ran down his body into his boots where they escaped through lace holes as steam.

'It is a duty to improve or enjoy, even the discharge of daily usefulness without which no man is fit for society. For fuck's sake, snap out of it.'

Now I could only answer my father with a look of despair, and endeavour to hide myself from his view behind a piece of cardboard from where I shouted, 'For fuck's sake I can't snap out of it.'

About this time we moved to a house at Belrive. This change was particularly agreeable as there was no rent to pay. Often, when the rest of the family retired for the night, I took the boat and passed many hours upon the water. It sprang a leak, and despite four hours of bailing out it sank. Another time I hoisted the sails and let the wind take me wherever it would. I ended up in France.

It took me two days of sailing to get back. Often I was tempted to plunge into the lake; that the waters might close over me and end my calamities forever, but each time I ran short of breath and had to surface. Thank heaven, it saved my life.

I lived in daily fear lest the monster whom I had created should perpetrate some new hobby like haddock stretching or nude woodchopping. None of these activities could obliterate the monster from my mind. I must find him, even if it means going to the Andes. There I would arrest him.

The monster would not leave my
  mind
Suppose he left it behind!
He could throw it in the sea
Dearie me
And that would be the end of me.

My father's health was deeply shaken by the horror of the recent events. We had to put heavy rocks on him to keep him still.

'When I reflect, my dear cousin,' said Elizabeth, 'I no longer see the world and its works as they before appeared to me. Before I looked upon the accounts of vice and injustice.'

'Don't worry, I will look up these accounts,' I said. I did, and there was a deficit of £50 10s 6d so we closed the books on that company.

'Yes,' I said, 'I felt she was innocent before she died. I felt her after she died and she felt innocent after she died. William and Justine were assassinated and the monster walks free, smoking fifty fags a day and God help the man who doesn't give them to him.'

'I would not change places with such a wretch,' she said.

'Well you certainly couldn't change places with him. You would need to be five feet taller and ten stone heavier.'

Elizabeth read my anguish in my countenance and kindly taking my hand threw it on the floor. She was so elegant it abolished any thought of using that one-eyed trouser snake.

Ah, the wounded deer dragging its fainting limbs to some untrodden brake, there to gaze upon the arrow which had pierced it and left it to die. Ah, if only a bowman would shoot an arrow into my leg, I could find an untrodden brake and, gazing at the arrow, die. [What a lot of bollocks! Ed.]

The high and snowy mountains were its immediate boundaries; but I saw no more ruined castles and fertile fields – only quite a few McDonald's. Immense glaciers approached the road from which I ran like fuck. I heard the rumbling thunder of the falling avalanche as it moved our house five hundred yards down the hill.

A tingling, long-lost sense of pleasure often came across me during the journey, as did some young woman who also came across. The very winds whispered in soothing accents – French, Italian, German and, believe it or not, Swahili. I spurred on my mule, striving to forget the world, my fears and my overdraft. Suddenly, as I was forgetting the world, my mule threw me and kicked me in the balls which swelled up like water melons and I had to carry them around in a wheelbarrow. The animal was trying to tell me something. Listening to the rushing of the Arve, which pursued its noisy way beneath, the same lulling sounds acted as a lullaby. I felt it as sleep crept over me as I, the mule and my swollen balls were down by the raging torrent.

We rest; a dream has power to poison
sleep.
We rise; one wand'ring though pollutes
the day.
We feel, conceive, or reason; laugh or
weep.
Three cheers, hip hip hooray.
It is the same for be it joy or sorrow,
The path of its departure still is free.
Man's yesterday may ne'er be like his
morrow;
Hi diddle diddle dee.

CHAPTER II

I spent the following day roaming through the valley. I stood beside the source of the Arveiron. The glacier with the slow pace is advancing down from the summit to barricade the valley and cut all the poor buggers off from the other side. The abrupt sides of the mountains were before me, but turning round suddenly they ended up behind me. The glorious Nature was broken only by the brawling waves, and from somewhere there came the sound of someone being sick. The thunder of the sound of a million tons of avalanche afforded me the greatest consolation. All I needed to cheer me up was a million tons of ice crashing down. The unstained snowy mountain top, the giant Alps – indeed all I need to make me sleep was the Swiss Alps and Mont Blancmange.

Where had they fled when the next morning I awoke? They had not fled anywhere. They were all still there. In fact, I need not have gone to sleep at all.

The next day my mule had its back legs shackled together to protect my balls. I resolved to ascend to the summit of Montanvert. I said to my groom, 'I resolve to ascend to the summit of Montanvert.'

He said, 'What you do is your business.'

The ascent revealed a scene terrifically desolate. In a thousand spots the traces of the winter avalanche may be perceived. Actually, I myself came out in a thousand spots and I was treated for youth's acne. The path, as you ascend higher, is intersected by ravines of snow, down which stones continually roll from above, crashing down on people's heads below. In fact, there was a whole generation of people with lumps on their heads. Apparently the lumps went through the families. The rain poured down from a dark sky and added to the melancholy impression. I myself could do a melancholy impression – the Hunchback of Notre Catford and the Hunchback of Marie Antoinette on the Gallows.

The field of ice is almost a league in width, but I spent nearly two hours falling down and getting up it. [Dear reader, I have a feeling he's going to meet the monster! Ed.] My heart which was before sorrowful, now swelled with something like joy. Actually, it was a mild coronary.

Suddenly nothing happened, but it happened suddenly. Mark you, I beheld the figure of a man advancing towards me with super-human speed; roughly, I would say he was doing 150 miles per hour. He bounded over the crevices over which I had walked with caution. His stature, as he approached, seemed to exceed that of man. I was troubled: a mist came over my eyes, nose and teeth and I felt a faintness seize me; but I was quickly restored by a bottle of 1909 brandy. I perceived as the shape came nearer (sight tremendous and abhorred!) that it was the wretch whom I had created. [God, he was slow recognising him! Ed.] Argggah! Yes folks, argggah! I trembled with rage and horror, resolving to wait his approach, and then close with him in mortal combat [for Christ's sake, don't!]. Again, his trousers were round his ankles.

'Ello, ave you got a fag?' he said.

'Devil!' I exclaimed, 'do you dare approach me? And do not you fear the fierce vengeance of my arm?'

'Oh don't be like dat, I only want a fag.'

It was the monster, argggah
He said, 'ave you got a fag?'
'No, I've only got an argggah'
'Alright, I'll have an argggah.'

'Be gone, vile insect [Eh?], or rather, stay that I may trample you to dust! And, oh! that I could, with the extinction of your miserable existence, restore those victims whom you have so diabolically murdered!

'Oh steady on, mate, I only done one. Now will you help me with my trousers.'

My rage was without bounds; I sprang on him, impelled by all the feelings which can arm one being against the existence of another. He hurled me 100 feet down a chasm and then he came down and helped me to my feet.

'Upsy daisy,' he said. 'Remember, thou hast made me more powerful than thyself, my height is superior to thine, my joints more supple, etc., etc. I could beat the shit out of you if I wanted. Now have you got a fag?'

'Here,' I said, 'here is a packet of twenty. That will be £2 and I sincerely hope you die of lung cancer.'

I hope you die of cancer
I will if I can sir
Personally I don't give a damn sir
I will smoke one hundred fags a
day
Until the cancer goes away.

So saying I helped his trousers up.

'Now remember that I am thy creature; I am thy Adam – but I am better dressed.'

'Begone! I will not hear you. There can be no community between you and me; we are enemies.'

Suddenly he pulled my trousers down. 'There, how do you like it?' he said. 'Let me turn up your trousers; one good turn deserves another.'

'I don't think it's a very good turn – if it was, it should be in the music hall.'

CHAPTER III

THE MONSTER'S TALE

'It was with considerable difficulty that I remember the original era of my being. By degrees, I remember, a stronger light pressed upon my nerves, so that I was obliged to shut my eyes. I walked over a cliff. By opening my eyes I found myself at the bottom of a cliff. Then I walked and I sought a place in the shade. This was the forest near Ingolstadt; and here I lay peacefully by the side of a brook, resting from my fatigue. A tree fell on me and I felt tormented by hunger and thirst. I ate some berries which I found hanging on the trees or lying on the ground. I slaked my thirst at the brook and then, lying down, I was overcome by sleep during which another tree fell on me. While I was under it some villagers asked for my autograph. A feeling of pain invaded me on all sides and I sat down and wept.

'Soon a gentle light stole over the heavens, and gave me a sensation of pleasure. I started up and beheld a radiant form rise from among the trees.[3] Of course, it was the moon! How silly of me not to recognise it. I was

[3]The moon [author's footnote].

still cold when under the trees I found a huge cloak; it had a ticket on it, 'Made in Taiwan', and I covered myself with it and became Chinese.

'My eyes became accustomed to the light and to perceive objects in their right forms; I could distinguish herbs from animals. I could tell the difference between a nettle and an elephant. One gave you a sting, the other killed you. I could tell hot from cold. One day I found a fire which had been left by wandering beggars and was overcome with delight at the warmth I experienced from it. In my joy I thrust my hand into the life embers [What a bloody fool! Ed.]. Food, however, became scarce and I often spent the whole day searching in vain for a few acorns, sausages or a leg of lamb.

CHAPTER IV

'I lay on my straw, but I could not sleep. I didn't know how to. I thought of the occurrences of the day. I remembered too well the treatment I had suffered the night before from the barbarous villagers who had driven me out. I remained quietly in my hovel, watching, and endeavouring to discover the motives which influenced their actions.

'The cottagers arose the next morning before the sun. A young woman arranged the cottage and prepared the food; the youth departed after the first meal, the greedy bugger.

'The young man was constantly employed out of doors, and the girl in various laborious occupations within. The old man I soon perceived to be blind as he kept walking into walls.

'A considerable period elapsed before I discovered one of the causes of the uneasiness of this amiable family – it was poverty. I discovered that because at dinner time they had no food on their plates. The two children suffered the pangs of hunger, for several times they placed food before the old man. They reserved none for themselves. He ate the lot, the greedy bugger.

'This trait of kindness moved me sensibly. I had been accustomed, during the night, to steal a part of their store for my own consumption [The shit! Ed.].

'I learned the names of the cottagers themselves. The girl was called 'Agatha', the youth 'Felix' and the man 'Father'. I cannot describe the delight I felt when I learned the ideas appropriated to each of these sounds, so I won't. I distinguished several other words without being able yet to understand, though I repeated them; such as 'fire', 'milk', 'bread', 'wood', 'shit'.

'Felix carried with pleasure to his sister the first little white flower that peeped out from beneath the snowy ground – she ate it.

CHAPTER V

'I shall relate events that impressed me with feelings which, from what I had been, have made me what I am. [Frankenstein made him what he am. Ed.]

'Spring advanced rapidly; the weather became fine but I did not. It was a surprise to me that what before was a desert was now a Kentucky Fried Chicken. I was refreshed by a thousand scenes of delight with a little crushed garlic. One night, mad with hunger, I killed all the staff and ate all the chickens. Colonel Sanders came along so I killed him as well.

'The old man played on his guitar. There was a tap on the door. Why any one would want to put a tap on a front door is hard to explain.

'It was a lady on horseback, accompanied by a countryman as a guide. The lady was dressed in a black suit, and covered with a thick black veil. Agatha asked a question, 'Are you a nigger?' The stranger only repeated the name of Felix. She held out her hand to Felix who kissed it and then spat on the floor. I could distinguish she was an Arabian so she was, in fact, a wog.

'She took the old man's guitar and sang delightful medleys:

'All nice girls like a sailor
All nice girls like a guitar
For there is something about a
   sailor
For you know what sailors are.'

'The wog's name was Safie but her entrance into my story and continuance is not important. Let me go to the day that all the children and Safie were out and the blind father was in the cottage.

CHAPTER VI

'I knocked on the cottage door.

' "Who's there?" said the old man.

' "Some one else," I said.

'I entered. "Pardon this intrusion," said I; "I am a traveller in want of a cigarette."

' "Enter," said De Lacey, "You will find some on the mantelpiece. Unfortunately, my children are away from home and, as I am blind, I am afraid I shall find it difficult to procure food for you."

' "Do not trouble yourself. I only need that and fire, milk, bread, wood and shit. Your children are kind – they are the most excellent creatures in the world; but unfortunately, they are prejudiced against me."

' "That is indeed unfortunate; but if you are blameless, can you not do something about it?"

' "I am ugly."

' "Can't you have plastic surgery? Barbara Cartland is going to have it."

'At that instant the cottage door opened and Felix, Safie and Agatha entered. "Quickly," he said, "I need fire, milk, bread, wood and shit!" Who can describe their horror and consternation on beholding me? Agatha fainted and Safie, unable to attend to her friend, rushed out of the cottage. Felix darted forward and with supernatural force tore me from his father, to whose knees I clung. In a transport of fury, he dashed me to the ground and attacked me violently with a crowbar. I could have torn him limb from limb as the lion rends the antelope. But my heart sunk within me as with bitter sickness. I quitted the cottage, and in the general tumult escaped unperceived to my hovel.

CHAPTER VII

'Cursed, cursed creator! Why did I live? I could with pleasure have destroyed the cottage and its inhabitants, and have glutted myself with their shrieks and misery. All I had to show was a pair of the blind man's knees.

'Sleep relieved me from the pain of reflection which was disturbed by the approach of a beautiful child who came running into the recess I had chosen. Suddenly, as I gazed on him, an idea seized me, that this little creature had lived too short a time to have imbibed a horror of deformity.

'Urged by this impulse, I seized him as he passed and drew him towards me. As soon as he beheld my form, he placed his hands before his eyes and uttered a shrill scream; I drew his hand forcibly from his face and said, "Child, what is the meaning of this? I do not intend to hurt you; listen to me."

'He struggled violently. "Let me go," he cried. "Monster! Ugly wretch! You wish to eat me and tear me to pieces – You are an ogre – let me go, or I will tell my papa. Hideous monster! Let me go. My papa, M. Frankenstein – he will punish you. You dare not keep me."

' "Frankenstein! you belong then to my enemy – to him towards whom I have sworn eternal revenge; you shall be my first victim."

'The child still struggled, and loaded me with epithets which carried despair to my heart; I grasped his throat to silence him, and in a moment he lay dead at my feet.

'I gazed on my victim, and my heart swelled with exultation and hellish triumph; clapping my hands, I exclaimed, "I too can create desolation; my enemy is not invulnerable; this death will carry despair to him, and a thousand other miseries shall torment and destroy him. Heh – heh – heh." '

CHAPTER VIII

'You must create a female for me – I need a shag – with whom I can live in the interchange of those sympathies necessary for my being. This you alone can do; and I demand it of you as a right which you must not refuse to concede. And have you got a fag?'

'I do refuse it,' I replied, 'and no torture shall ever extort a consent or a cigarette from me.'

'You are in the wrong,' replied the monster, 'and, instead of threatening, I am content to reason with you. I am malicious because I am miserable. Not only that, I am gasping for a fag and a fuck. If you consent, neither you nor any other human being shall ever see us again: I will go to the vast wilds of South America. My food is not that of man; I do not destroy the lamb and the kid to glut my appetite; trees, acorns and berries afford me sufficient nourishment. I am a vegetarian. My companion will be of the same nature as myself, and will be content with the same fare. We shall make our bed of dried leaves; the sun will shine on us as on man, and it will ripen our food while we are screwing on the leaves.'

'I consent to your demand, on your solemn oath to quit Europe forever.'

'I swear,' he cried, 'by the sun and the blue sky of Heaven, and by the fire of love that burns in my heart [that only left the moon], if you grant my wish you will never behold me again. I shall go to Bexhill-on-Sea; anybody who goes there is never seen again.'

Suddenly, he quitted me, fearful perhaps of any change in my sentiments. I saw him descend the mountain – with greater speed than the flight of an eagle – at 100 miles per hour, and quickly lost sight of him among the undulations of the sea of ice.

The labour of winding among the little paths of the mountain and fixing my feet firmly as I advanced perplexed me; still I kept going arse over tip. By the time I had gone 250 arse over tips, night was far advanced. I came to the halfway resting place and seated myself beside the fountain. The wind blew it all over me and I got soaked. The stars shone at intervals, the dark pines rose before me and here and there a broken tree lay on the ground – and I did arse over tips over them. Clasping my hands in agony, I exclaimed, 'Oh! stars and clouds and winds, and four Dispirins, do take the pain away.'

I cannot describe to you how the eternal twinkling of the stars weighed upon me, so I won't. I listened to every blast of wind – blast! blast! it went as it blew the fountains all over me again.

Morning dawned before I arrived at the village of Chamonix soaking wet and with hyperthermia. I took no rest, but returned immediately to Geneva. Even in my own head I could give no expression to my sensations – they weighed on me with a mountain's weight, and the result was I had to walk bent double. Thus, I returned home, and entering the house presented myself to my family bent double with mountains. My haggard and wild appearance awoke intense alarm. They called the fire brigade; I would answer no questions from the fire brigade. 'Are you on fire?' they said. 'No,' I said. With pulleys they removed the mountains off my back; I was able to stand straight for the first time in three days.

VOLUME THREE

CHAPTER I

Day after day, week after week passed away, as did my Granny. On my return to Geneva I could not collect the courage to re-commence my work. I feared the vengeance of the disappointed fiend and his grieving for a wife and cigarettes. I could not compose a female without again devoting several months to profound study and laborious disquisition. My father saw the improvement in me and turned his thoughts towards the best method of eradicating the remains of my melancholy: he recommended an audience with the Pope but he was too busy and sent a bottle of Holy Water which I drank – it gave me typhoid.

It was after this that my father called me aside and thus addressed me: 'Victor Frankenstein, 10 Le Grande Rue, Geneva, Switzerland.' I wonder if I ever got that. It was marked 'Return to Sender, Not Known Here.'

'I am happy to remark, my dear son, that apart from your typhoid you have resumed your former pleasures and seem to be returning to yourself. Where from I do not know, but you seem to be returning. My son, you seem still unhappy; like yesterday, you never finished up your spotted dick. You know how ideal spotted dick is for people with typhoid.'

I trembled violently at his exordium, which he played brilliantly, and my father continued:

'I confess, my son, I have always looked forward to your marriage with dear Elizabeth.'

Oh fuck, now he was trying to marry me off. There were no ends he wouldn't go to get rid of me.

'You were attached to her from your early infancy by a chain.'

'My dear father, my future hopes and prospects are entirely bound up in the expectation of our union, that is The Tradesmen and Miners.'

I remember also the necessity imposed upon me of journeying to England and studying at the Bexhill-on-Sea Body Building Centre. I must absent myself from all I loved while thus employed in creating a female monster. Putting a pair of boobs in place would be a good start.

At Bexhill-on-Sea there was a morgue where they had the bits I needed. It was the city of the aged where many of the limbs would fall off in the street. These I would gather after dark. I was capable of taking pleasure in the idea of such a journey. My father hoped that the change of scene would restore me entirely to myself. Finally he talked me down from my position on top of the cupboard.

I now made arrangments for my journey to Bexhill-on-Sea. One of them was Chopin's E^{b} Nocturne for the spoons. In the time given it was the best arrangment I could do.

We travelled at the time of the vintage and heard the song of the labourers. I lay at the bottom of the boat in the hold under the luggage where I could be alone from that chatterbox Clerval. As we drifted down the Rhine we saw groups of labourers who had been hiding behind the trees from their work. Oh, surely the inhabitants would retire to the inaccessible peaks of the mountains where they hurl themselves to death rather than pay income tax.

Clerval! Even now it delights me to record your words – unending bloody yakking. He was a being formed in the very poetry of nature: it would take him two bloody hours to describe a tree. His soul overflowed with ardent affections and his friendship was of that devoted and wondrous nature. it is just that he would never stop bloody yakking. To satisfy his eager mind he took up kung fu.

And where does he now exist? [He doesn't, he snuffed it. Ed.] Is this gentle and lovely being lost forever? [Yes. Ed.] Has his mind perished? [Yes. Ed.] does it only exist in our memory? [Yes, if you want it to. Ed.] His favourite poem:

> The sounding cataract
> Haunted him like a passion: the
> tall rock,
> The mountain, and the deep and
> gloomy wood,
> Their colours and their forms,
> were then to him
> An appetite; a feeling, and a love,
> That had no need of a remoter
> charm
> By thought supplied, or any
> interest
> Unborrow'd from the eye.[4]

[4]Wordsworth's *Tintern Abbey* [author's footnote].

We arrived at Rotterdam; it was a clear morning. At length we arrived in England where we saw the numerous steeples of London – St Paul's, the Tower, Angus Steak House, Deep Pan Pizza, Boots, The London Dungeons, Garfunkels . . .

CHAPTER II

London was our present point of rest; we were determined to remain several months in Neasden for Clerval to study Hindus. This wonderful city desired the intercourse of men of genius. They were fishmongers, plumbers, bricklayers, green grocers and King Edward. Company was irksome to me, especially A Company of the Irish Guards.

Clerval's design was to visit India, in the belief that he had in his knowledge of its various languages, starvation, plague and leprosy. And he believed in trade – importing chicken vindaloo and exporting fish and chips. I tried to conceal myself as much as possible and I wore a clown's mask. I often refused to accompany him, alleging another engagement like mud wrestling. I had finally found a good pair of boobs to start on my female monster.

We received a letter from a person in Scotland; that is, it had no stamp on it. He mentioned the beauties of his native country – Rangers and haggis and bagpipes and whisky. Clerval was eager to accept the invitation and I wished to view again mountains and streams. I packed up my chemical instruments and bits of body. I'd finish my labours in some obscure nook in the northern highlands of Scotland. To blend with the natives around I wore a kilt and, following tradition, under it I wore nothing. Every morning, to make sure, I stood on a mirror. We saw a quantity of game and herds of stately deer, which tasted delicious.

We visited the tomb of the illustrious Hampden and the field on which that patriot fell – he tripped over a stone.

To my horror I discovered the monster had followed me and he said, 'Have you finished her yet? Hurry up, I want a shag.'

To keep out the wind, I wore an ankle length kilt.

On an island there were three miserable huts, and eighteen miserable tenants. One of these tenants was vacant. One of the tenancies was also vacant. It contained two rooms and these exhibited all the squalidness of the most miserable penury. The thatch had fallen in, the neighbours had fallen out; I ordered it to be repaired. The walls were unplastered and the door was off its hinges. The cottagers had been benumbed by want and squalid poverty. When they spoke their brains hurt and they fainted to the floor.

It was a monotonous yet ever-changing scene. Its hills are covered with veins, as were the legs of the islanders. Starting my experiments, my mind fixed on the consummation of my labour and my eyes shut to the horror of my proceedings. Thus, I kept walking into the walls. I looked towards the completion of my work with tremendous hope which I dared not trust myself to question but which was intermixed with obscure forebodings of evil that made my heart sicken in my bosom. [What a lot of bollocks! Ed.]

CHAPTER III

One evening the moon was just rising from the sea, dripping wet. I trembled, and my heart failed within me. [Where else? Ed.] Looking up I saw by the light of the moon the daemon at the casement with his ghastly grin. He had followed me in my travels; he had swum the English Channel. He had swum up the Thames to Scotland. He stubbed his cigarette out on the roof. His wife-to-be was in bits – her boobs were on the cases, her legs on the floor and her bum on the table.

Several hours passed, and three buses, while I remained at the window gazing out to sea. A fisherman called out. 'Och ter mukty.' 'Fuck you too,' I replied. I was hardly conscious of extreme profundity, until my ear was suddenly arrested by the sound of the local police. They took my ear to the police station where it was questioned and finally released.

Back home, I heard footsteps along the passage, the door opened and the wretch appeared.

'You have destroyed the work which you began; what is it that you intend?'

'I intend to sweep it up in the morning,' I replied.

'Don't you dare break your promise to me,' he said. 'I

have endured toil and misery. I left Switzerland with you and crept along the shores of the Rhine. I swam the English Channel and I've swum the stinking Thames.'

'Begone! I do break my promise; never will I create another like yourself. I gave you cigarettes; what more do you want?'

The monster saw my determination and knashed his teeth at speed; they sounded like castanets. To make a living, he'd been on exhibition in the circus as the ugliest man in the world.

'I have journeyed the Sandy McNab desert,' he said. 'It was small compared with the Sahara. How in heavens I survived it I do not know; it was a miracle of survival.'

'Leave me, I am inexorable.'

'It is well I go, but remember – I shall be with you on your wedding night.'

In a few moments I saw him in his boat, which shot across the waters at a 100 miles per hour with an arrowy swiftness and was soon lost amidst the waves.

All was again silent, but his words rang in my ears; 'ding-a-ling, ding-a-ling' they went. I burned with rage; smoke billowed from my shirt. The trouble was, I could not swim at a 100 miles per hour. Why had I not followed him and closed with him in mortal strife. Because he would have beat the shit out of me. I shuddered to think who might be the next victim to be sacrificed to his insatiate revenge – some poor bloody crofter would suddenly find himself being hurled over a cliff. I resolved to fall before my enemy without a bitter struggle.

Leaving thoughts of my bride, I went for a walk along the shore. When it became noon I lay down on the grass, and was overpowered by a deep sleep. I awoke to find I had been washed out to sea; I was a mile from the shore.

Napoleon had gathered his army
for Moscow
To his assistance I must go
When we got to Moscow it was on
fire
So we all had to retire
The British arrested Napoleon and
to him couldn't be meaner
They imprisoned him on St
Helena.

Coming ashore, I received a letter which recalled me to life and I determined to quit my island at the expiration of two days. Yet before I departed there was a task to perform, on which I shuddered to reflect. I must pack up my instruments – my thermoreck, my buzzometer, my nauseaometer and the small porcelain statue of a milk-maid. The next morning, at daybreak, I summoned sufficient courage and unlocked the doors of my laboratory. The remains of the half-finished creature, whom I had destroyed, lay scattered on the floor. She was everywhere. I paused to collect myself, then I collected her. With trembling hands and revolving knees I conveyed the instruments out of the room. I put all the apparatus, and bits of the woman, in a basket.

Between two and three in the morning the moon rose, and so did I; then, putting my basket aboard a little skiff with a great quantity of stones and some ham sandwiches, I sailed four miles offshore. At one time the moon, which had before been clear, was suddenly overspread by a thick cloud, and I took advantage of the moment of darkness to cast my basket into the sea – and also to eat my ham sandwiches. Having reached the shore, I slept soundly, awakening every now and then to eat another ham sandwich. As there were twelve, they kept me awake until the morning.

I pushed the boat from the shore. The wind was north-east, and must have driven me far from the coast. I looked upon the sea; it was to be my grave. 'Fiend,' I exclaimed, 'your task is already fulfilled!' For some reason I thought of Elizabeth; I thought of my father and of Clerval and also of the 3rd BN Irish Guards.

Some hours passed thus; but by degrees the sun declined away into a gentle breeze and the sea became free from the breakers. Mind you, from the age of this boat it should have been at the breakers a long time ago. Suddenly, I saw a line of high land towards the south.

The dreadful suspense I had endured for several hours suddenly caused a flood of tears to gush from my eyes which started to fill the boat and I had to bail out. I resolved to steer directly towards the town as a place where I could most easily procure nourishment, beans on toast and Horlicks. Fortunately, I had money with me, money which I would invest as soon as I was ashore.

I addressed some of the natives. 'My good friends, would you be so kind as to tell me the name of this town and a bank where I can invest my money.'

'You will know that soon enough,' replied a man with a hoarse voice – so I offered him a throat pastille. 'Maybe this town will not prove to your taste.'

I did not understand. So far I had not tasted anything. I was surprised to receive so rude an answer from a stranger. I was disconcerted at the frowning and angry countenances of his companions. 'Why do you answer me so roughly?' I replied. 'I want my throat pastille back.'

'I do not know,' said the man, 'what the custom of the English may be, but it is the custom of the Irish to hate villains.'

Oh fuck! I had ended up in Ireland. I perceived the crowd rapidly increase from six to 10,000.

A man said, 'Begorra! you must follow me to Mr Kirwin's, to give an account of yourself.'

'My account? Why? It stands at £102 overdrawn. Is that a crime in this country?'

CHAPTER IV

I was soon introduced into the presence of the magistrate. He looked upon me, however, with some degree of severity. At college he had taken a degree in Severity. He asked for witnesses.

About half a dozen men came forward and collided. One had landed a boat on the shore the night before. It was very dark and he had to walk alongside his boat. He walked, taking parts of the fishing catch – in this case a whale which filled the boat – and that is why he had to walk alongside. As he was proceeding up the beach, he struck his foot against something and fell full length; they found that he had fallen on the body of a man.

The first part of his deposition did not in the least interest me, but when the mark of the fingers was mentioned I remembered the murder of my brother and felt myself extremely agitated; my limbs trembled and a mist came over my eyes obscuring my face. The magistrate observed me and propped me up with his walking stick.

I entered the room where the corpse lay, and was led up to the coffin. How can I describe my sensations on beholding it? I feel yet parched with horror. When I saw the lifeless form of Henry Clerval stretched before me I gasped for breath and threw myself on the body, managing to climb out just in time before they nailed the lid on. My friend Clerval, my friend, my benefactor, and monumental bore.

The human frame could no longer support the agonies that I endured; some bits of me fell off. I was carried out of the room in convulsions – the bits of me that were left.

A fever succeeded to this. I lay for two months on the point of death; my ravings, as I afterwards heard, were frightful. I said 'fuck' eighteen times. Fortunately, I spoke my native language.

Why did I not die? [Yes, why didn't you? Ed.] But I was doomed to live and in two months I found myself as awaking from a dream, stretched out on a wretched bed surrounded by gaolers, chains, turnkeys, bolts and a pot. When I looked around and saw the windows and the squalidness of the room in which I was, all flashed across my memory. I was in the nick; I groaned bitterly.

This disturbed an old crone who was sleeping in the chair beside me. She was a hired nurse. 'For Christ's sake, shet up!' she said. I think she meant 'Shut up', I have no idea what 'shet up' meant. She seemed to characterise that class who travel Economy on Spanish airlines. Her face was a mass of criss-crossed lines that spelt 'arseholes'.

'Are you better now?' she said.

I replied in the same creep language, with a feeble voice, 'I believe that I am still alive to feel this misery and horror.'

'For that matter,' replied the crone, 'if you mean about the gentleman you murdered, I think hanging will end all your suffering.'

I turned with loathing from the woman who could

utter so unfeeling a speech to a person just saved yet on the very edge of death. I was unable to reflect on all that had passed – six trams, twelve buses and four dust carts. My temperature went up to 190° and they had to switch on the air conditioning.

There was no one near me with a gentle voice of love; no dear hand to support me with a bottle of Liebfraumilch. The physician came and prescribed medicines. The old woman prepared them for me; but utter carelessness was visible in the first. Who could be interested in the fate of a murderer, but the hangman who would gain his fee? He charged £1 for every pound of body weight. For me he would get £14. When he came he wore ear plugs. His visits were short – they lasted three minutes.

Occasionally, a friendly gaoler would give me a bottle of Liebfraumilch. Such were my thoughts when Mr Kirwin entered. He expressed sympathy; he spoke, '*Votre chat denotre tante est dans le jardin.*'

Then he said, 'Can I make things better for you?'

I said, '*Oui*, would you like to book *une chambre* at the Savoy Hotel for me?'

He replied, 'I am sorry, the Savoy Hotel don't take gaol birds.'

'I mean after the hanging.'

He replied, 'The Savoy Hotel don't take dead people.'

Mr Kirwin went on to say, 'Immediately upon your being taken ill, all the papers that were on your person were brought to me, *the Daily Mail*, *The Times* and *the News of The World*. I found several letters, all from the Midland Bank asking for you to clear your overdraft of £100. But you are ill, even now you are trembling; you are unfit for agitation of any kind.'

How many types of agitation are there?

'Your family is perfectly well,' said Mr Kirwin, 'and a friend has come to visit you.'

'Oh take him away. I cannot see him, for God's sake; do not let him enter.'

'I should have thought, young man, that the presence of your father would have been welcome!'

'My father!' I cried. 'Why the fuck didn't you say?'

Nothing at this moment could have given me greater pleasure than the arrival of my father. I stretched out my hand to him.

'Are you, then, safe – and Elizabeth – and Ernest? Did you manage to avoid that big tax demand?' I said.

'Why are you dwelling in this terrible prison?'

'Well, they will not let me stay at the Savoy.'

'And poor Clerval, what a terrible end.'

The name of my unfortunate friend was too great to be endured and I shed tears. Soon the cell was ankle deep in tears.

'Alas! yes, my father, the most horrible things hang over me; a noose for a start. I should have died on the coffin of Henry.'

'Then why didn't you if it would have made you feel better?'

Mr Kirwin came in, and insisted that my strength should not be exhausted by too much exertion. The appearance of my father in flowing white robes was like that of an angel complete with wings, and he flew away.

I sat for hours, motionless and speechless, wishing for some mighty revolution that might bury me and my destroyer. I sat for three days waiting; still the mighty revolution did not come.

I was obliged to travel nearly a 100 miles to where the

court was held – so I had plenty of time before it arrived. I was spared the disgrace of appearing publicly as a criminal: I gave evidence from the clothes cupboard, speaking through the keyhole. The grand jury rejected the bill (I had but one in for expenses) on it being proved that I was on the Orkney Islands at the hour that the body of my friend was found; and a fortnight after my removal, I was liberated from prison.

My father was enraptured on finding me freed from the vexations of a criminal charge. What he meant was, murderer! I was again allowed to breathe the fresh atmosphere. He had booked a room for me at the Savoy. They took me to an optician who could find nothing wrong with my eyes so I went to a cobblers. He said he could find nothing wrong except that I needed a pair of new shoes.

One morning, my father awoke me with an electric cattle prod. I was in a deep depression. At night I put a loaded pistol by my bed but in the morning it was still there, and so was I.

My father was concerned for my health. I was a shattered wreck; I lay in bits all over the cabin floor. My strength was gone – I think it went to Bexhill-on-Sea. I was a mere skeleton. I urged our leaving Ireland and we took our passage on the SS *Plassey*, a splendid ship with a slight tendency to sink. It was midnight. I lay on the deck looking at the stars, with the passers-by walking over me.

I repassed my life, the death of my mother and my departure for Ingolstadt where I became a compulsive onanist. I called to mind the night in which my monster asked for a cigarette.

I had been in the custom of taking every night a small

quantity of laudanum – yeah, man! I now doubled my usual quantity. My dreams presented a thousand objects that scared me: dentist's drill, hand grenade, hangman's rope, a bank overdraft, cuddly toy, a set of golf clubs, electric toaster, holiday for two in Venice, dishwasher, a dozen wine glasses . . . Next morning, they threw a bucket of water over me. The fiend was not here; he must have been there! A sense of security, a feeling that a truce was established, and a disastrous future imparted itself to me. In other words, I was shit scared.

CHAPTER V

The voyage came to an end and I found I had overtaxed my strength. I discovered I could only travel on a stretcher or by walking on one leg. My father wished me to seek amusement in society. I abhorred the face of man. How they would, each and all, abhor me and hunt me from the world for what I had done. Arghhhh!

At length, my father yielded to my desire to avoid society and he locked me in the W.C., where I had a plentiful supply of water. He would say to me through the keyhole, 'You can take a horse to water but he needn't drink; you can't make a silk purse out of a sow's ear; a bird in the hand is worth two in the bush; beware your sins will find you out; a stitch in time saves nine.'

'Thank you father' said I.

'I continued in the same dream world. I imagined I was the Greek god Apollo, surrounded by woodland nymphs. Then, one day, I was no longer Apollo but Victor Frankenstein and strapped down to the bed. Was there any mail when I was away? Yes.

The day before we left Paris (how in God's name did I get there?) I received the following letter from Elizabeth:

My dear friend,

It gave me the greatest pleasure to receive a letter and your dirty laundry and you are no longer at a formidable distance like Ireland but still wear the restrictive jacket. How you must suffer! I hope to see you looking even more ill than when you quitted Geneva. This winter has been miserable, tortured as I have been by revolving swannicles and anxious suspense; yet I hope to see peace in your countenance and to find that your heart is not totally void of comfort and tranquillity. I know you enjoy so much being ill.

P.S. Perhaps on our wedding day you can leave off your straitjacket.

Elizabeth Lavenza
Geneva, May 18th, 17—.

After the ceremony was performed, a large party assembled. The sun was hot so we did not touch it. The sun sank lower in the heavens; and we passed the river Drance. We looked at the numerous fish that were swimming in the clear water so, stripping off, I dove into the water and retrieved a fish which I gave to my Elizabeth who straightaway ate it.

CHAPTER VI

We walked on the shore, enjoying the transitory light and dogs crapping on the beach. Suddenly a heavy storm descended and we were drenched. I had been calm during the day; now, between my teeth I clenched a dagger. In my left hand I carried a grenade, while in my right hand I had a sword.

I earnestly entreated Elizabeth to retire, resolving to join her as soon as I had some knowledge of the whereabouts of the monster. She left me and went to prepare divorce papers. One of the hand grenades was in my trouser pocket. Should it suddenly explode, I would be castrated on my wedding night.

Suddenly I heard a shrill and dreadful scream. I could feel the blood trickling in my veins, and tingling in the extremities of my limbs. This state lasted but for an instant; the scream was repeated, and I rushed into the room.

Great God! why did I not then expire? [Nothing was stopping you. Ed.] She was there, lifeless and inanimate, thrown across the bed, her head hanging down, her body hanging up and her pale and distorted features half covered by her hair. Everywhere I turn I see the same figure – £10,000 from her insurance.

There lay the body of Elizabeth, my love, my wife, so lately living, so dear, so worthy, so dead! Deadly languor and coldness of the limbs told me that rigor mortis had set in. What I now held in my arms had ceased to exist. No, now she was a stiff.

I looked up and saw at the open window a figure, the most hideous and abhorred. A grin was on the face of the monster which seemed to take in part of his chest. He seemed to jeer, the cheeky devil. With his fiendish fingers he reached towards the package of my cigarettes, which he grabbed. Drawing my pistol from my bosom, I fired and the recoil threw me back and jammed me in the window. He plunged into the lake and swam away with the swiftness of lightning.

The discharge of my pistol brought a crowd into the room and the ceiling down. I pointed to the spot from where he had disappeared. We followed the tracks with maps and boats, and nets were cast – but all we caught was a fourteen-pound salmon. After passing several hours, we returned hopeless but with a good catch of fish.

After having landed, they proceeded to search the country; search parties going in different directions among the woods and vines following a trail of dog-ends. We never saw any of them again. I attempted to accompany them, and proceeded a short distance from the house; but my head whirled around and ended up facing the other way. My steps were like those of a drunken man and I fell at last in a state of utter exhaustion. In this state I was carried back and placed on a bed, hardly conscious of what had happened. My eyes wandered round the room and eventually returned to me.

After an interval I arose and, as if by instinct, crawled across the room; many thought I was a dog and patted me. There in the room, the corpse of my beloved lay. There were women weeping around; I hung over her boobs but gradually I slid off. I joined my sad tears to theirs and soon the room was ankle deep in tears.

I knew not whether my friends and my cigarettes were safe from the malignity of the fiend; my father even now might be writhing under his grasp and threatening him with the police. Who knows? Ernest might be dead at his feet. King Edward might be trampled underfoot. I started up and resolved to return to Geneva with all possible speed. There were no horses to be procured, so instead we boiled some eggs.

However, it was hardly morning, and I might reasonably hope to arrive by night. I hired men to row and took an oar myself because I always experienced relief from mental torment by bodily exercise. But the overflowing misery I now felt, and the excess agitation that I endured, rendered me incapable of any exertion. I threw down the oar and, leaning my head upon my hands, tears streamed from my eyes which flooded the boat and we had to try to bail out. I saw the fish play in the waters as they had done a few hours before; they had then been observed by Elizabeth. In memory of her, I stripped and dived in and retrieved a fish, and in memory of her, I ate it. The sun might shine, or the clouds might lower, but nothing could appear to me as it had done the day before. A fiend had snatched from me every hope of future happiness, plus twenty cigarettes: no creature in the history of man had ever been so miserable as I was then. Mind you, that might be a bit of an exaggeration. Mine had been a tale of hirror and horror. I have reached their acme, and what I must now relate can be tedious to you. [It's all been bloody tedious. Ed.]

My father and Ernest yet lived, but the former sunk under the tidings that I bore. We threw him a life belt. His Elizabeth, his more-than-daughter, whom he doted on; in fact she was a mass of dote marks. But alas, the springs of existence suddenly gave way: he was unable to rise from his bed and in a few days he died in the arms of his bank manager who, at the last gasp, got him to pay his overdraft.

What then became of me? I know not; and I asked somebody what had become of me; they said I became a train. I lost sensation, and chains and darkness were the only objects that pressed upon me. Sometimes I dreamed that I wandered in flowery meadows and pleasant vales with the friends of my youth, but I awoke and found myself in a public toilet. I gained a clear conception of my miseries and situation and was then released from my prison because they called me mad as a result of me saying I was Julius Caesar and was on my way to invade England and become a director of Hansons.

I began to reflect on the reason why I thought I was a Chinese junk. I think it was the monster whom I had created. I was possessed by a maddening rage when I thought of him and I prayed that I might have him within my grasp; I would tie grenades to his balls and explode them.

I began to reflect on the best means of securing him, and for this purpose I repaired to a criminal judge in the town and told him that I had an accusation to make – that I knew the destroyer of my wife, and who had stolen my fags.

The magistrate listened with attention and kindness. At this stage he signalled two attendants who rushed forward and put me in a straitjacket. As I spoke, rage sparkled in my eyes; the magistrate was intimidated: 'You are mistaken,' said he, stifling a laugh. 'I will exert myself; and if it is in my power to seize the monster, I shall.' He was laughing, with tears running down his cheeks.

They confined me to a padded cell, so I started to devote my life to the destruction of this monster. But to the magistrate, this elevation of mind had much the appearance of madness. He endeavoured to sooth me as a nurse does a child, pushing me in a pram and giving me a milk bottle.

'Man,' I cried, 'how ignorant art thou in thy pride of wisdom! Cease; you know not what it is you say.' They remembered it and let me free, and for a while I became an amateur hangman. I hanged seven amateur murderers.

CHAPTER VII

Then my situation was one in which all voluntary thoughts were swallowed up and lost, and I never found them again. I looked everywhere. I was hurried away by fury, revenge and an overdraft. I provided myself with a sum of money together with a few jewels which belonged to my mother. I took them as she slept – God bless her!

And now my wanderings began, which are to cease but with life. I have traversed a great portion of the earth using an American Express card. How I lived I hardly know – mainly bank jobs. I have stretched my failing limbs upon the sandy plain and have been crapped on by an elephant; rangers dug me out. I have swum the stormy seas; the Dover life boat saved me. I have searched the deepest; a rescue team got me out. But revenge kept me alive. I dare not die, that is the last thing I should do. I would never rest until I had exploded his balls and fed them to my dog.

That night, I knelt by the grave of my father and my wife. I kissed the earth – it tasted fucking terrible – and then exclaimed, 'By the sacred earth on which I kneel, by the shades that wander near me, by the deep and eternal grief that I feel, I swear (I also drink and smoke) to pursue the daemon until he or I shall perish in mortal conflict, preferably him. And I call on you, spirits of the dead – just don't answer all together.'

Then, to my horror, I heard the monster. He addressed me in an audible voice; that is why I could hear it: 'I am satisfied, miserable wretch! You have determined to live, and I am satisfied.'

I darted towards the spot from which the sound proceeded; it was a spot about six inches in diameter, but the devil eluded my grasp. The moon shone full upon his ghastly and distorted shape as he fled with more than mortal speed – 100 miles per hour.

I pursued him, guided by a trail of cigarette ends. I saw the feared fiend enter by night and hide himself in a vessel bound for the Black Sea. Just my luck, I took the wrong sea; I was colour blind. He took passage for the Red Sea, so he escaped.

Amidst the wilds of Tartary and Russia, he still evaded me. Sometimes the peasants, scared by this horrid apparition, informed me of his path; sometimes he himself, who feared that if I lost all trace of him I should despair and die. I saw the print of his huge footstep on the snowy plain, and I fell in it. A spirit of good followed and directed my steps, and I fell down a coal hole. I survived in the deserts by making a camel fricassee; it took me a week to eat it.

In other places, human beings were seldom seen, and I survived on elephant vindaloo. To gain the friendship of the villagers, I distributed some food – I shot an ant which I made into a stew.

I was still hell-bent on catching the monster. I exchanged my land-sledge for one fashioned for the inequalities of the frozen ocean. Immense and rugged mountains of ice often barred up my passage; it was very painful to have ice block up your passage.

Once, after my sledge-dogs had conveyed me up to the summit of an incredibly sloped mountain, one, sinking under his fatigue, died – I ate him. Suddenly, my eyes caught a dark speck upon the dusky plain. I strained my sight to discover what it could be; it was indeed a dark speck on the dusky plain.

Oh: with what a burning gush did warm tears fill my eyes. I caught the tears in a saucepan and before they became cold I made a cup of Oxo. Yes, my sledge-dogs were wonderful. They never stopped to urinate, but raised one leg and did it with the other three legs running.

In this manner, many appalling hours passed. Several of my dogs died and I made them into sausages which I enjoyed. I saw your vessel riding at anchor, and holding forth to me hopes of succour and life. I quickly destroyed part of my sledge to construct oars; and by these means was enabled, with infinite fatigue, to move to your ship.

Walton, in continuation.
August 26th, 17—.

You have read this strange and terrific story, Margaret, and do you not feel your blood congeal with horror? If it does, you must see a doctor. Sometimes, seized with sudden agony, he could not continue his tale; at others, his voice broke – he kept the pieces in a small bag. His face would suddenly change to an expression of the wildest rage as he shrieked out imprecations at his persecutor, so we put the straitjacket on him.

Sometimes, I endeavoured to gain from Frankenstein

the particulars of his creature's formation – where he got the bits.

'Are you mad, my friend?' said he. 'Whither does your senseless curiosity lead you? Is it to the monster's balls which I intend to explode?'

Thus had a week passed away, but he had not. Frankenstein discovered that I made notes concerning his history; he played them back to me on his violin. I have listened to the strangest tale that ever imagination formed; much more frightening than *Midsummer Night's Dream*. To soothe him, I drained an entire bottle of brandy down his throat which seemed to relax him. In fact, it relaxed him to the point where he couldn't get out of bed. He talks of beings who visit him from regions of a remote world. They are all a bit loony.

'When younger,' said he, 'I believed myself destined for some great enterprise, like a shareholder in Lloyds. My imagination was vivid, yet my powers of analysis and application were intense. I had conceived the idea, and executed the creation, of a man who would strangle people. I wasn't very pleased with that – or the people he strangled.

September 5th, 17—.

My beloved sister,
We are surrounded by mountains of ice; the cold is excessive. Many of my unfortunate comrades have already found a grave. They go frozen stiff, so we cast them over the side. Frankenstein has daily declined in health. Three times in the last week he has nearly died. He suddenly has feverish fire in his eyes; but he is exhausted, and when suddenly roused to any exertion

he speedily sinks again into apparent lifelessness. We throw buckets of water over him.

The ship is immured in ice, we are all shit scared and the crew want to mutiny. When Frankenstein heard this he addressed them with a courageous speech. He encouarged them to be brave and that their hearts be strong and their spirits become heroic. With that he sang 'God Save the Queen'.

He was willing to risk the lives of every sailor in an endeavour to catch his monster. What a prick! The leader of the sailors said that Frankenstein was a cunt: 'Listen to him and we'll all fucking snuff it.'

My chief intention was occupied by my unfortunate guest, a more unfortunate guest I've yet to have, whose illness increases by degrees and he is entirely confined to his bed and needs a po, but his aim was so appalling that urine went everywhere except in the chamber.

September 7th, 17—.

The die is cast; I have consented to return – if we are not first destroyed.

September 12th, 17—.

There was a shout of tumultuous joy. Frankenstein asked what the shout was. 'They shout,' I said, 'because they will soon return to England.'

'Do you really return?'

'Alas! yes. I cannot withstand their demands. I cannot lead them unwillingly to danger, and I must return. They have threatened me with fifty lashes, then being hung from the yardarm, keelhauled and made to walk the plank and swallow the anchor; fuck that.'

'You may give up your purpose, but mine is assigned to me by Heaven.' Shouting this, he sprang from his bed straight into the po, but the exertion was too much for him. He fell back and fainted, the silly sod.

At length, he opened his eyes; he breathed with difficulty. In the meantime, he told me he had not many hours to live. Quickly, I telegraphed an insurance policy on his life with Lloyds.

To make life difficult, Frankenstein revived. I waited patiently for him to die again but, alas, he raved on endlessly about the monster. At length, exhausted by his effort, he sunk into silence. About half an hour afterwards, he attempted again to speak, but he wasn't very clear.

Margaret, what comment can I make on the untimely extinction of this glorious spirit? What can I say that will enable you to understand the depth of my sorrow? Unfortunately, all he has left behind is a cabin reeking of stale urine.

Great God! what a scene has just taken place! I entered the cabin where lay my ill-fated friend. Over him hung a form which I cannot find words to describe: gigantic in stature, yet uncouth and distorted. As he hung over Frankenstein, he heard the sound of my approach; he sprang towards the porthole and got stuck half way. I called on him to stay for beans on toast and Horlicks.

He paused, turning towards the immobile form of his creator. He seemed to forget my presence; in return I forgot his. His voice seemed suffocated: 'I did – did it, uuh, I deaded him, your missus. I am saying sorry, Frank.'

Not noticing, Frankenstein attached two grenades to

the monster's balls that exploded, blowing the monster's balls to smithereens. The cabin was speckled with bits of monster balls.

'Eureka!' shouted Frankenstein.

'Elizabeth, I killed her for her fags. Yes, I done Frank's wife in, but he tore my woman to bits. At least his wife is still in one piece. My wife's bits are in a basket at the bottom of the sea. Oh give me a fag,' he said as he snatched the packet from my hand and then stuffed six of them in his mouth. 'I'll have dat beans on toast now while I run over the frightful catalogue of my sins, which are on sale at all good book shops; oh bugger! this cabin stinks of piss; let's go up on deck.'

The monster cast a last glance at Frankenstein. 'He's snuffing it. It couldn't have happened to a nicer man. But soon,' he cried, 'I shall die and what I now feel is no longer felt. Soon these miseries will be extinct. I shall ascend my funeral pile triumphantly smoking the best Virginia cigarettes, and exult in the agony of the torturing flames. If they get too bad, I'll call the fire brigade. The light of the conflagration will fade away; my ashes will be swept into the sea by the winds. My spirit will sleep in peace.'

He sprang from the window upon the ice-raft which lay close to the vessel. He was soon borne away by the waves, and lost in darkness and distance.

I descended to the cabin. I shook Frankenstein. 'Wake up, Frank! You can stop pretending to be dead; he's gone!'

THE END